Hieroglyphics

Arthur Machen

Hieroglyphics

The present edition is a reproduction of previous publication of this classic work. Minor typographical errors may have been corrected without note; however, for an authentic reading experience the spelling, punctuation, and capitalization have been retained from the original text.

ISBN: 978-1-63637-254-9

TABLE OF CONTENTS

NOTE

It was my privilege, many years ago, to make the acquaintance of the obscure literary hermit, whose talk I have tried to reproduce in the pages that follow. Our first meeting was one of those chance affairs that now and then mitigate the loneliness of the London streets, and a second hazard led to the discovery that we had many interests in common. I think that the Hermit (as I shall call him) had begun to find the perpetual solitude of his years a growing terror, and he was not sorry to have a listener; at first, indeed, he talked almost with the joy of a child, or rather of a prisoner who has escaped from the house of silence, but as he chose subjects which have always interested me intensely, he gave as much pleasure as he received, and I became an assiduous visitor of his cell.

He had found an odd retreat. He avoided personalities, and had a happy knack of forgetting any that I vouchsafed on my side, (he forgot my name three times on the first evening that we spent together, and succeeded in repeating this feat over and over again since then), and I never gathered much of his past history. But I believe that "something had happened" many years before, in the prehistoric age of the 'seventies. There had been a break of some sort in the man's life when he was quite young; and so he had left the world and gone to Barnsbury, an almost mythical region lying between Pentonville and the Caledonian Road. Here, in the most retired street of that retired quarter, he occupied two rooms on the ground floor of a big, mouldy house, standing apart from the street and sheltered by gaunt grown trees and ancient shrubs; and just beside the dim and dusty window of the sitting-room a laburnum had cast a green stain on the decaying wall. The laburnum had grown wild, like all the trees and shrubs, and some of its black, straggling boughs brushed the pane, and of dark, windy nights while we sat together and talked of art and life we would be startled by the sudden violence with which those branches beat angrily upon the glass.

The room seemed always dark. I suppose that the house had been built in the early eighteenth century, and had been altered and added to at various periods, with a final "doing up" for the comparative luxury of someone in the 'tens or 'twenties; there were, I think, twenty rooms in it, and my friend used to declare that when a new servant came she spent many months in finding her way in the complicated maze of stairs and passages, and that the landlady even was now and then at fault. But the room in which we sat was hung with flock paper, of a deep and heavy crimson colour, and even on bright summer evenings the crimson looked almost black, and seemed to cast a shadow into the room. Often we sat there till the veritable darkness came, and each could scarcely see the white of the other's face, and then my friend would light two lonely candles on the mantelpiece, or if he wished to read he set one on a table beside him; and when the candles were lighted I thought that the gloom grew more intense, and looking through the uncurtained window one could not see even the friendly twinkle of the gas-lamp in the street, but only the vague growth of the laburnum, and the tangle of boughs beyond.

It was a large room and gave me always a sense of empty space. Against one wall stood a heavy bookcase, with glass doors, solid and of dark mahogany, but made in the intermediate period that came between Chippendale and the modern school of machine-turned rubbish. In the duskiest corner of the room there was a secretaire of better workmanship, and two small tables and three gaunt chairs made up the furnishing. The Hermit would sometimes pace up and down in the void centre of the room as he talked, and if I chanced to be sitting by the window, his shape would almost disappear as he neared the secretaire on his march, and I heard the voice, and used to wonder for a moment whether the man had not vanished for ever, having been resolved into the shadows about him.

I have spent many evenings in that old mouldering room, where, when we were silent for an instant, the inanimate matter about us found a voice, and the decaying beams murmured together, and a vague sound might come from the cellars underneath. And it always seemed to me as if the crypt-like odour of the cellar rose also into the room, mingling with a faint suggestion of incense, though I am sure that my friend never burned it. Here then, with such surroundings as I have indicated, we held our sessions and talked freely and with enjoyment of many curious things, which, as the Hermit would say, had the huge merit of interesting no one but ourselves.

He would sometimes, whimsically, compare himself to Coleridge, and I think that he often deliberately talked in S. T. C.'s manner with delight in the joke. For, I need hardly say that the comparison was not in any way a serious one; he had a veneration for Coleridge's achievement, with a still greater veneration for that which Coleridge might have achieved, which would have caused him to regard any such comparison, seriously entertained, as unspeakably ludicrous. Still, he liked to regard himself as a very humble disciple in Coleridge's school, he was fond, as I have said, of imitating his master's manner as well as he could, and I think that he cherished, in the fashion of S. T. C., the notion that he had a "system," an esoteric philosophy of things; he sought for a key that would open, and a lamp that would enlighten all the dark treasure-houses of the Universe, and sometimes he believed that he held both the Key and the Lamp in his hands.

It is a confession of mysticism, but I incline to think that he was right in this belief. I recall the presence of that hollow, echoing room, the atmosphere with its subtle suggestion of incense sweetening the dank odours of the cellar, and the tone of the voice speaking to me, and I believe that once or twice we both saw visions, and some glimpse at least of certain eternal, ineffable Shapes. But these matters, the more esoteric doctrines of "the system" have entered hardly or not at all into the very imperfect and fragmentary notes that I have made of his conversations on literature.

I should scarcely be justified in calling him a literary monomaniac. But it is true that Art in general, and the art of literature in particular had for him a very high significance and interest; and he was always ready to defend the thesis that, all the arts being glorious, the literary art was the most glorious and wonderful of all. He reverenced music, but he was firm in maintaining that in perfect lyrical poetry there is the subtlest and most beautiful melody in the world.

I can scarcely say whether he wrote much himself. He would speak of stories on which he was engaged, but I have never seen his name on publishers' lists, and I do not think that he had adopted a pseudonym. One evening, I remember, I came in a little before my accustomed time, and in the shadowy corner of the room, a drawer in the secretaire was open, and I thought that it looked full of neat manuscripts. But I never spoke to him about his literary work; and I noticed that he did not much care to talk of literature from the commercial standpoint.

It is perhaps needless to say that I consulted my friend before publishing these notes of his conversations. I had been forced to leave London for some months, and I wrote to him from the country, requesting his permission to give to the world (if the world would have them) those judgments on books which I had listened to in Barnsbury. His reply allowed me to take my own way, "with all my heart, so long as you make me sufficiently apocryphal. I am not going to compete with 'real' critics whose names are printed in the papers; but if you can maintain the incognito and allow your readers (supposing their existence) to believe that I am a mere figment of your brain, you can print my obiter dicta 'with ease of body and rest of reins.' Here is a suggestion for a title: what do you say to 'Boswell in Barnsbury'? But I really had no notion that you were taking notes all the time. Remember: keep the secret, and the secrets."

I regarded this as a very liberal license, and I have tried to set in the best order I could compass the "system" so far as it relates to letters. I do not pretend that I am a verbatim reporter, for I had to trust to my memory, and though I tried to arrange my notes at the time, I fear I have fallen here and there into confusion. Still, I think that the six chapters which follow will seem fairly consecutive in their argument and arrangement, and the "Appendix"—a confession of failure—is, in reality, the result of the "cyclical mode of discoursing," in which the Hermit jocularly professed to follow Coleridge.

Perhaps indeed Coleridge was deceived, and my dear friend with him, in the hope of real essential knowledge; but even so, these fragments which I propose are evidence that the latter earnestly desired the truth and sought it.

A. M.

HIEROGLYPHICS

I

Do you know that just before you came in I found something highly significant in the evening paper? I am afraid from your expression that you rather undervalue the influence of the press; indeed, I remember one day when we were out together you swore at an inoffensive boy who tried to allure us with news of all the winners. I think I pointed out at the time that even horse-racing and an interest in "events" are preferable to stagnation, and that there is something august in the universal human passion for gambling. And, after all, the office-boy who "puts on" half-a-crown is really only an example of the love of man for the unknown; the half-crown is a venture into mystery, with that due flavour of commercialism which we in England add to most of our interests. But you see, don't you? that gambling, even under its most sordid aspects, is not altogether sordid; it's the mystery, the uncertainty, the hours of "strange surmise" that the smallest bet gives to the bettor that make the real delight of betting. When the office-boy wins and gets ten shillings for the risk of his two-and-six, his delight is not by any means pure love of gain, it is distinguished by a very marked line from the constantly repeated joys of the grocer, who is always buying delicious tea at ninepence and selling it at one-and-six. Here you have commercialism in its simplest form; but our office-boy, though he likes the money well enough, stands on a much higher plane. For the moment he is the man who has succeeded in solving the enigma of the Sphinx, in discovering the unknown continent, in reading the cypher, in guessing at the song the Sirens sang, in unveiling the hidden treasure that the buccaneers buried on the lonely shore; he has ventured successfully into the dim region of surmises. And when he loses, there are always consolations; the Indies have not been discovered on this voyage, certainly, but there have been wonders on the way, he has enjoyed many hours of delicious expectation. The proof that he likes the sport, even when he loses, is that he invariably takes the first opportunity of venturing again in the same manner. And, by the way, perhaps I was a little severe just now on trade, and especially on the grocer's sugary and soapy enterprise. Perhaps if we were to look with a rather finer vision into the commercial spirit, we might find that it is not wholly commercial, not altogether sordid. Of course if the grocer opens his shop with a certainty, mathematical or almost mathematical, that the public will buy his wares, he is a wicked fellow; he is gambling with loaded dice, betting against a horse that he knows is to be made "all right," playing cards with honours up his sleeve, and I am sure that if this be his enterprise, it will always meet with our sternest disapproval. Casanova died towards the close of the last century, and since then cardsharping has become impossible to a man of taste. But seriously, I suspect that a good deal of the allurement that trade possesses for so many of us is the risk which it almost always implies, and risk means uncertainty, and uncertainty connotes the unknown. So you see our despised grocer turns out, after all, to be of the kin of Columbus, of the treasure-seekers, and mystery-mongers, and delvers after hidden things spiritual and material. I suppose we have here the real explanation of the human trading passion, and the solution of a problem that has often puzzled me. The problem I mean is this: how does it happen that the English are both the greatest poets and the greatest tradesmen of the modern world? Superficially, it seems that keeping shops and making poetry are incompatibles, and Wordsworth and Coleridge, Keats and Shelley, Tennyson and Poe, should have come from Provence or Sicily, from the "unpractical," uncommercial Latin races. But if we trace back the trading instinct to that love of a risk—or in other words to the desire for the unknown—the antinomy disappears, and it will become perfectly natural that the race which has gone to the world's end with its merchandise, has penetrated so gloriously into the further regions of poetry.

But that reminds me of what I was saying just after you had lit your pipe. I think I remarked that I had seen something of very high significance in the evening paper, and the glare of disgust with which you greeted my observation constituted an interruption, and an interruption that had to be dealt with. Now again you seem to hint at doubt with your eyebrows; you would say, perhaps, that I have not made out a very convincing case for journalism? But you must remember that my mental process resembles that of Coleridge; you called on the Seer at eleven o'clock in the morning, and (if young and imprudent) asked him a question. And at the waning of the light Coleridge was still diligently engaged in answering your question for you, having talked without intermission all the summer day. A "cyclical mode of discoursing" the pious Henry Nelson Coleridge called it, and he deals faithfully with certain persons who complained "that they could get no answer to a question from Coleridge." And you will please to remember this when you think that I am "wandering"—a vice of which Coleridge also was accused. To-night, for example, on the evening paper being mentioned, your face expressed disgust and contempt, which I diagnosed (and rightly, I believe?) as a tribute to the enormous interest taken by the editors of these agreeable journals in the very latest sporting news; an interest which allows

3

but little space for the discussion of pure literature. Hence my remarks on the gambling-spirit; and now I hope you will at least assume a thrill of interest when the boy bawls in your ear "All the winners and S. P." It is possible you may be thinking of Ulysses or of Keats at the moment, and the interruption may annoy you, but it will do so no longer when you reflect that a burning anxiety as to the running of Bolter is for many thousands the symbol—and the only possible symbol—of the Doom of Troy and the wandering fields of foam, and the Isle of Calypso, and the "strange surmise" of Pizarro and all his men.

But here is the evening-paper in question. Yes, the colour is, perhaps, a little sickly. A kind of pinky-green, it seems, doesn't it? But it forced itself on my notice in the most extraordinary manner, and I expect you will have to admit, when you have heard the story, that some Powers were at work. Well, I was walking up and down the room, just as it was getting dusk, and every now and then I stopped and looked out of the window. Yes, I was making phrases as usual, and thinking of a new story in the middle of the old one: hence the quarter-deck exercise. I daresay you have remarked that I do not keep my window in a very brilliant condition, and the air this evening, you will remember, was rather misty—October, I always think, wears a peculiar dim grace in Barnsbury—so I hope you will not find my impressions too incredible. I was staring, then, out of the window, when to my vast astonishment, a great pale bird seemed suddenly to shoot up into the air from the road, and to flutter into the garden, where it became entangled in that sapless old laburnum that weeps green tears upon the wall. I saw, as I thought, the beating and fluttering of wings, and I ran out, imagining that I was to secure a strange companion for my solitude. It was the evening paper, not a bird, and I saw at once that it would be impious to let it flutter there unread, so I secured it and brought it in, meditating the adventure, and wondering what strange message was thus borne to my eyes. So I went through its columns patiently, even to the leaderettes, and I will do myself the justice to say that I at once recognised the communication that was addressed to me in this singular and even I may say Arabian fashion. It was a short comment upon some agitation that is now appealing rather strongly to Progressive leaders; but the subject-matter is of no consequence, since the significance lies in the last sentence. Here it is: "We are glad to hear that extensive arrangements have been made for the dissemination of literature."

You don't see the immense importance of that? You surprise me. Let us go into it, then. I told you I was not very precise as to the exact scope of the agitation alluded to—it may be a question of a heavy tax on persons who will say "lady" instead of "lydy," it may be an affair of restricting the franchise to citizens thoroughly ignorant of history; it doesn't matter—but here are men who wish some political change to be effected, and these men are issuing printed matter, the purpose of which is to convince others of the righteousness of this particular "program." And this printed matter is called "literature." You know the sort of thing indicated. It may be a series of arguments, simple and fallacious, it may be in dialogue, it may be in story form, it may assume the guise of parody, it may be a brief history. And now what I want to know is this: here we have a vast body of thought, clothed in words, ranging from the agreeable leaflets that we have been speaking of up to—let us say—the Odyssey, and all this mass is known as literature: what is to be our criterion, our means of distinguishing between the two extremes I have mentioned and all the innumerable links between them? Is the whole mass literature in the true sense of the word? If

5

not, with what instrument, by what rule are we to divide the true from the false, to judge exactly in the case of any particular book whether it is literature or not? Of course you may say that the question is rather verbal than real; that "literature" is a general term conveniently applied to anything in print, and that in practice everybody knows the difference between a political pamphlet and the Odyssey. I very much doubt whether people do understand precisely the distinction between the two, but for the avoidance of verbal confusion I suggest that when we mean literature in its highest sense we shall say (for the present at all events), "fine literature"; and the question will be, then: what is it that differentiates fine literature from a number of grammatical, or partly grammatical, sentences arranged in a more or less logical order? Why is the Odyssey to come in, why is the "literature" of our evening paper to be kept out? And again, to put the question in a more subtle form: to which class do the works of Jane Austen belong? Is "Pride and Prejudice" to stand on the Odyssey shelf, or to lie in the pamphlet drawer? Where is Pope's place? Is he to be set in the class of Keats? If not, for what reason? What is the rank of Dickens, of Thackeray, of George Eliot, of Hawthorne; and in a word, how are we to sort out, as it were, this huge multitude of names, giving to each one his proper rank and station?

I am glad it strikes you as a big question: to me it seems the question, the question which covers the final dogma of literary criticism. Of course after we have answered this prerogative riddle, there will be other questions, almost without end, classes, and sub-classes of infinite analysis. But this will be detail; while the question I have propounded is the question of first principles; it marks the parting of two ways, and in a manner, it asks itself not only of literature, but of life, but of philosophy, but of religion. What is the line, then; the mark of division which is to separate spoken, or written, or printed thought into two great genera?

Well, as you may have guessed, I have my solution, and I like it none the less, because the word of the enigma seems to me actually but a single word. Yes, for me the answer comes with the one word, Ecstasy. If ecstasy be present, then I say there is fine literature, if it be absent, then, in spite of all the cleverness, all the talents, all the workmanship and observation and dexterity you may show me, then, I think, we have a product (possibly a very interesting one), which is not fine literature.

Of course you will allow me to contradict myself, or rather, to amplify myself before we begin to discuss the matter fully. I said my answer was the word, ecstasy; I still say so, but I may remark that I have chosen this word as the representative of many. Substitute, if you like, rapture, beauty, adoration, wonder, awe, mystery, sense of the unknown, desire for the unknown. All and each will convey what I mean; for some particular case one term may be more appropriate than another, but in every case there will be that withdrawal from the common life and the common consciousness which justifies my choice of "ecstasy" as the best symbol of my meaning. I claim, then, that here we have the touchstone which will infallibly separate the higher from the lower in literature, which will range the innumerable multitude of books in two great divisions, which can be applied with equal justice to a Greek drama, an eighteenth century novelist, and a modern poet, to an epic in twelve books, and to a lyric in twelve lines. I will convince you of my belief in my own nostrum by a bold experiment: here is Pickwick and here is Vanity Fair; the one regarded as a popular "comic" book, the other as a serious masterpiece, showing vast insight into human character; and applying my test, I set Pickwick beside the Odyssey, and Vanity Fair on top of the political pamphlet.

I will not argue the matter at the moment; I would merely caution you against supposing that I imply any equality of merit in the books that I have thus summarily "bracketed." You mustn't suppose that I think Dickens's book as good as Homer's, or that I have any doubts as to the vast superiority of Vanity Fair over all the pamphlets in the world. "Here is a temple, here is a tub," we may suppose a child to say, learning from a picture-alphabet; but the temple may be a miserably designed structure, in ruinous condition, and the tub is, perhaps, a miracle of excellent workmanship. But one means worship and the other means washing, and that is the distinction. Or, to take a better example; the bottom boy in the sixth form may be a miserable dunce compared with the top boy in the fifth; still the dunce is in the sixth form, and the genius is in the fifth. Or, to take a third instance (I want you to understand what I'm driving at), the fact that an English orator is fluent, brilliant, profound, convincing, while a Greek orator is stuttering, stupid, shallow, illogical does not hinder that the former, though he may speak ever so well, still speaks English, while the latter, however badly he may speak, speaks in Greek for all that. Analogies, as you know, are never perfect, and must not be pressed too far; they suggest rather than prove; but I hope you understand me though you may not agree with me.

But before we argue the merits of my own literary solvent, we might very well see what we can do with other tests. I daresay you can suggest a good many. We won't go into the question of printed and not printed, written or not written, because it is obvious that the visible symbols by which literature is recorded have nothing to do with literature itself. In the beginning all literature was a matter of improvisation or recitation and memory, and hieroglyphics, writing, printing are mere conveniences. Indeed the point is only worth mentioning because there are, I believe, simple souls who think that the invention of printing has some sort of mysterious connection with the birth of literature, and that the abolition of the paper duty was its coming of age. But I don't think we need trouble ourselves much about a view of literary art which regards the cheap press as its father and the school board as its nursing mother. Many people think, on the other hand, that literature is to be estimated by its effect on the emotions, by the shock which it gives to the system. You may say that a book which interests you so intensely that you cannot put it down, that affects you so acutely that you weep, that amuses you so immensely that you roar with laughter must be very good. I don't object to "very good," but from my point of view, "very good" and "fine literature" are two different things. You see I believe that the difference between interesting, exciting, tear-compelling, laughter-moving reading matter and fine art is not specific but generic: who would blaspheme against good bitter beer, who would say that because it is good, it is therefore Burgundy?

I am not quite sure that I am not muddling up two things which are in reality distinct. I mean I am in doubt whether the faculty of making the reader cry ought not to be distinguished from the faculty of interesting him intensely. On the whole I think that it would be well to draw a line between the two, especially as "interesting" is somewhat ambiguous.

And you think it a paradox, then, to maintain that the power of exciting the emotions to a high degree is not a mark of fine literature? But just think it over. Suppose that a few yards from this room—in the next house, in the next street—a woman is waiting for the return of her husband and son. A ring comes at the bell, there's a reddish-brown envelope, and inside it the message: "Railway accident father killed." Well, you can imagine the effect that these four words will have on the woman's emotions; she will either faint away, or burst into an agony of tears; she may even die of the shock, and you can't have a more striking emotional result than death, can you? Very well; but is the telegram fine art? Is it art? Is it even artifice? It isn't art because it is true! But if I invented such a telegram and sent it to a woman whose husband and son were away, would it thereby become art? You must see perfectly well that it would be nothing of the kind; and I must ask you to explain how a book which is, virtually, a long succession of such telegrams can rise higher than its origin and source? You must see, I think, that the question of truth and falsity can make no real difference to our (no doubt pompous) high æsthetic standpoint; and if you admit that four words which produce an emotional result are not necessarily art, then it follows that four hundred or four hundred thousand words woven together on the same principle are in no better position. An increased quantity means no doubt an increased artifice, but artifice and art are very different things. We may agree then that it is impossible to measure the artistic merit of a book by the emotional shock that it may give to its readers. I have never read the "Sorrows of Werther"; but if you have read it and it has made you sorrowful you are hereby warned against deducing from this effect any conclusion as to its æsthetic value.

I confess all this seems A B C to me, though I see you are still inclined to think me a little paradoxical—not to say sophistical—but it grows more difficult when one gets to the question of the "interesting" or "absorbing" book. As I said "interesting" seems such an ambiguous word. It may stand for that æsthetic emotion produced, say, by the Œdipus; it may denote the wide-eyed attention of the butcher's wife listening to the story of my landlady as to the love-affairs of the grocer's daughter—and there are many books which are, virtually, "Tales of My Landlady" printed and bound. We must really then omit "interesting" in our account of the possible criteria of fine art; the word as it were cancels itself out, because it may mean on the one hand the possession of the highest artistic value, or on the other it may serve as epithet for a book which gratifies the lowest curiosity. You know there are books which the French have kindly named "romans à clef"; and I suppose there is no more miserable form of book-making. The receipt is easy enough. The grocer's daughter, to whose amours I alluded just now, is really named Miss Buggins, and the gentleman is Mr Tibb. Well, suppose that my landlady, relating their lyric to the butcher's wife, should, with a knowing wink, profess to tell the story of Miss Ruggins and Mr Ribb—she would simply be composing a roman à clef without knowing it. You might say that it is hardly worth while to labour the point, that such "interest" as this is wholly and lamentably inartistic—that it is the very contrary to all true art—but it is not long since a person of some literary note, in criticising the "Heptameron," stated that its chief value lay in the fact that one could identify the persons who tell the stories and those also of whom they were told!

But there is another interest of a much higher kind, and that is the sensational. We have done some excellent books of this sort in England, and perhaps you will understand the class I mean when I say that a novel of this description is hard to lay down, and harder still to take up again when you have once found out the secret. This is not high art; you are always at liberty to put down "Lycidas," but then you are compelled to take it up again and again, and the secret of "Lycidas" is always a secret, and one never fails to experience the joy of an artistic surprise. Still the books I mean sometimes show very high artifice, and in itself, perhaps, the quality that I am talking about, the power of exciting a vivid curiosity, an earnest desire to know what is to come next is not, like the vulgar roman à clef curiosity, in actual disaccord from the purpose of art. Indeed I imagine that this trick of stimulating the curiosity may be made subservient to purely æsthetic ends, it may become a handmaid to lead one towards that desire of the unknown which I think was one of the synonyms I gave you for the master word — Ecstasy. Still, though the trick is a good one, it will not, by itself, make fine art. You may discover so much by reading the "Moonstone," that monument of ingenuity and absurdity. On the face of it all detective stories come under this heading: formally, no doubt, they must all be reckoned as tricks, and they may vary from the infinitely ingenious to the infinitely imbecile, and so far as I remember, the famous French tales of detection verge towards the lower rather than the higher ground. But I am inclined, not very logically, perhaps, to make an exception in favour of Poe's Dupin, and to place him almost in the sphere of pure literature. Logically, he is a detective, but I almost think that in his case the detective is a symbol of the mystagogue. As I say, I should be pressed hard if I were asked to make out my case in terms and syllogisms, but if you require me to do so, I would say first of all that the atmosphere of Dupin — and you must remember that in literature everything counts; it is not alone the plot, or the style that we have to consider — has to me hints of that presence which I have called ecstasy. Listen to this:

"It was a freak of fancy in my friend (for what else shall I call it?) to be enamoured of the Night for her own sake; and into this bizarrerie, as into all his others, I quietly fell; giving myself up to his wild whims with a perfect abandon. The sable divinity would not herself dwell with us always; but we could counterfeit her presence. At the first dawn of the morning we closed all the massive shutters of our old building; lighting a couple of tapers which, strongly perfumed, threw out only the ghastliest and feeblest of rays. By the aid of these we then buried our souls in dreams—reading, writing, or conversing, until warned by the clock of the advent of the true Darkness. Then we sallied forth into the streets, arm in arm, continuing the topics of the day, or roaming far and wide until a late hour, seeking amid the wild lights and shadows of the populous city, that infinity of mental excitement which quiet observation can afford."

And again; in the stories themselves, in the conduct of M. Dupin's detective processes, I find a faint suggestion of the under-consciousness or other consciousness of man, a mere hint, not, I think, expressed in so many words, rather latent than patent, that if you would thoroughly understand the rational man you must have sounded the irrational man, the mysterious companion that walks beside each one of us on the earthly journey. Of course the artifice in the Dupin stories is of the very highest kind, but for the reasons I have given I am inclined to think that there is more than artifice, and the shadow, at all events, of art itself.

But this exceptional case of Poe's detective tales only leads us back to the main proposition—that the power of exciting a very high sensational interest does not, in itself, mark out a book as being fine literature. I think I proved the proposition by my instance of the "Moonstone," but if that does not convince you, we might demonstrate this theorem in the same way as we demonstrated the other one about the "literature" that produces its effect on the emotions. We have only to send out a series of telegrams, or we may even glance at the newspaper, and follow a case in the Central Criminal Court. Or we may affirm, more generally, that life often offers many highly absorbing and highly interesting spectacles, but that life is not art, and therefore, that literature which fails to rise above the level of life, or rather, to penetrate beneath the surface of life, is not fine literature in our sense of that term. A gold nugget may be as pure and fine as you like, but it is not a sovereign; it lacks the stamp; and it is the business of art to give its stamp and imprint to the matter of life.

I really think then that we have disposed of perhaps the most generally received of artistic fallacies—that books are to be judged by their power of reproducing in the reader those feelings of grief, interest, curiosity, and so forth which he experiences or may experience in his everyday life, which he really does experience in greater or less degree every time he talks to a friend, takes up a newspaper, or receives a telegram. It comes to this again and again, doesn't it, that Art and Life are two different spheres, and that the Artist with a capital A is not a clever photographer who understands selection in a greater or less degree.

But before we go on with our work and see what can be done with other literary "solvents" I want to make a digression. I should have made it before, if you had pulled me up at the proper cue, and that was when I spoke of "interest" as a highly ambiguous term, the fruitful parent of "undistributed middles." You see how the unscrupulous sophist would bend this word to his dark work, don't you? It would be, I suppose, something like this:

A very high degree of interest [of the artistic kind] is the mark of fine literature.

But, the "Moonstone" excites a very high degree of interest [of the sensational kind].

Therefore, the "Moonstone" has the mark of fine literature.

You note the "paltering" with the word, its use now in one sense, and now in another; and if that sort of thing were allowed we should have Wilkie Collins placed among the Immortals before we knew where we were. But hasn't it occurred to you that nearly all the terms we are using are patient of the same vile uses? You remember that we began with "literature" itself, as a monstrous example of ambiguity, sheltering as it did both the publications of the Anti-Everything Society and the Song of Ulysses' Wandering; even now we are trying to track the monster to his den in spite of his manifold turnings and disguises. In the meanwhile, for the sake of clearness, we agreed to prefix the epithet "fine" to the word when we meant the "Odyssey" class, though if we say "fine" so often I am afraid we run the risk of being thought superfine. However one must run all risks in the cause of making oneself understood; and so I say you ought to have pulled me up when I talked about "art" and "books that appealed to the emotions." My "art" may not be the same as your "art," and "emotions" are still more dangerous in the same way.

I think I made some attempt to deal with "art" as I was talking. I contrasted it with "artifice," and my phrase "Artist with a big A" was another hint to you that the word must be handled cautiously. You know that in ordinary conversation we say that bees have "the art" or "an art" of making hexagonal cells of wax, that wasps have an art of making a sort of paper for their nests, that there is an art of logic, an art of cookery, an art in making a gravel path. Now in each of these instances the word really speaks of the adaptation of means

15

to ends. In the case of the bees and wasps there is a slightly different nuance of meaning, because they make their cells and their paper just as a bird builds its nest, through the influence of forces which to us are occult, which we conveniently sum up under the word instinct. In the arts of cookery and pathmaking there is a conscious employment of certain means towards the securing of certain ends; and it is at least possible that the swallow, gathering its materials and shaping them, has at the moment nothing but a blind impulse, similar to that of hunger—we all know when we are hungry and we all know what to do in such a case, but we do not all know the physiology of the stomach and the gastric juices, and perhaps not one of us knows the whole secret of inanition and nutrition. We simply eat because we want to eat, not because we wish to supply ourselves with a certain quantity of peptones; and so perhaps the swallow gathers her nest and shapes it, without the consciousness of the eggs and the little birds that are to follow. But I need not remind you that there are plenty of well authenticated instances of animals who have consciously used means to secure ends, and thus "art" in its common significance is not even an exclusively human faculty. When, for example, the bees find themselves in danger of being left queenless, they administer what has been called "royal food" to a common grub, and that which would have been a worker becomes a queen; and in this case the bees are as much "artists" as the cook who puts a particular ingredient into a dish with the view of obtaining a particular flavour.

Now, then, let us apply all this to our matter. I daresay you have often heard a book praised for its "great art," and if you have read it you will have discovered that its "art" is simply contrivance, the very adaptation of means to ends that we have been discussing.

16

"The art with which the mystery is carefully kept in the background," "the art by which the two characters are contrasted throughout the volume," "the highly artistic manner in which Fernando and the heroine are brought together on the last page"— these, you see clearly, are contrivances, artifices, in no way differing in degree from the contrivances of the man who makes the garden path, of the cook who "dusts in" just a suspicion of lemon-rind, of the bee who administers the "royal food." This "art" then is a totally different thing from our Art with the capital letter, with the epithet "fine," or "high" before it; and in future when I mean "adaptation of means to ends," I shall always say "artifice"; while "art" will be retained and set apart for higher uses.

And now as to "emotion." Here, I think, you ought to have been down on me. You might have said: "You declare that the appeal to the emotions is not a test of fine literature. But to what then does Homer appeal? What is the "Œdipus" but an appeal to the emotions? What is all exquisite lyric poetry but the cry of the emotions, set to music?" I suppose that, as a matter of fact, you understood my real meaning by the instance I gave; the anguish of a wife at the loss of a husband; you saw that what I wanted to say was this: that fine literature does not content itself with repeating, or mimicking, the emotions of private, personal, everyday life. Still, I should have gone into the matter more fully then, and as I did not do so, we had better see what can be done now. And do you know that I believe that the best approach we can make to a rather subtle question will be a somewhat indirect one? Just now I was talking about Poe's Dupin stories, and I tried, rather vaguely, to justify my tentative inclusion of them in the higher class of letters, by pointing out that Poe seemed to hint at the "other-consciousness" of man, and to suggest, at least, the presence of that shadowy, unknown, or half-known companion who walks beside each one of us all our days. I tried to realise the image of a man, followed or rather attended, by a spiritual fellow, treading a path parallel with but different from his own; and now I want you to carry out this image into the sphere of words. Already you must have a hint of it. One might draw a figure; something like this:

Fine Literature.	"Literature."
Art.	Artifice.
Emotion.	Feelings.

And before I go into the special question, let me extend the list; it will explain itself.

Romance, romantic.	A "Romantic" Affair in the West End.
Tragedy, tragic.	"Tragedy" in Soho.
Drama, dramatic.	Le "drame" de la Rue Cochon: "Dramatic" Elopement in Peckham.
Interest, interesting [of "Hamlet"].	An "interesting" number of "Snippets."
Lyric.	The "Lyric" Theatre.
Inebriated.	In an "inebriated" condition.

That almost gives my secret away, doesn't it? Of course you see the place that the words in the right-hand column take in the scheme. The "Romantic" Affair in the West End really concerned the life of a draper's assistant, who robbed his master's till, in order that he might make presents to Miss Claire Tilbury, one of the "Sisters Tilbury" now performing at the "Lucifer." An unmentionable person cut his throat in some alley off Greek Street; hence the "Tragedy" in Soho. Two peculiarly squalid servants, who beat out their master's brains, under singularly uninteresting circumstances, acted the "Drama" of the Rue Cochon, and it was a dissolute barmaid who eloped "dramatically" from Peckham in the dog-cart of her employer. The two varying uses of the word "lyric" need not be underlined for you, who know the Elizabethans and the Cavaliers; but perhaps I may say that he who tastes calix meus inebrians will not be in an "inebriated" condition. It would be possible to extend these parallel columns almost to infinity; but I think the list is long enough for our purpose, and "Trench on Words" is a well-known handbook. But you see my right-hand column word, parallel with "Emotion"? You see I have written "Feelings," and I suggest that it will be convenient to speak of feelings when we mean the things of life, of society, of personal and private relationship, while we may reserve emotion for the influence produced in man by fine art. Thus it will be with emotion that we witness the fall of Œdipus, the madness of Lear, while we feel for our friends and ourselves in misfortune. That seems to make it plain enough, doesn't it; you see now, clearly, what I mean by saying that the power of producing an emotional shock cannot be a test of fine literature. Art must appeal to emotion, and sometimes, no doubt, with a shock; but it must always be to the emotion of the left-hand column, never to the "feelings" on the right hand. So you must never tell me that a book is fine art because it made you, or somebody else, cry; your tears are, emphatically, not evidence in the court of Fine Literature.

I daresay it may have struck you that the tests we have considered hitherto have been, in the main, popular tests. No doubt many persons calling themselves critics have praised the art of a book because it has drawn tears from eyes, or because it has not suffered itself to be put down, or because it contains easily recognisable portraits of well-known people, but such critics are to be spelt with a very small initial letter, and, as I said, I don't think we want to extend that list of parallels. There is another test that I had forgotten: I suppose there really are people who believe that a book is fine "because it will do good," but I don't think we'll argue with them, though I once knew a liberally-educated man who said a certain book was fine because it tended "to raise one's opinion of the clergy." So we will reckon our "popular" tests as done with, and proceed to the more technical solvents that are proposed by professed men of letters.

Three of these more literary criteria occur to me at the moment, and I believe we shall understand them and the position which they represent better if we take them, at first, at all events, in a mass. I can conceive, then, that many persons whose opinion one would respect would state their position in literary criticism somewhat as follows:—"If a book (they would say) shows keenness of observation, insight into character, with fidelity to life as the result of these capacities; if its art (we should say, artifice) in the design and 'laying out' of the plot, in the contrivance of incident is confessedly admirable, and finally if it is written in a good style: then you have fine literature. Fine art, in short, is a clear mirror, and the artist's skill consists in arranging and selecting such parts of life as he thinks best for his purpose of reflection."

Well, now, as to the first point: fidelity to life, clearness of reflection, the selection being taken for granted, as no one out of an asylum would maintain that a book must mirror the whole of life, or even the millionth part of one particular man's life. Come, let us apply the test in question to one or two of the acknowledged excellencies—to the "Odyssey" for instance, to the "Morte D'Arthur," to "Don Quixote." Is the story of Ulysses, in any accepted sense of the phrase "faithful" to life as we know it? Is it "faithful," that is to say, with the fidelity of Jane Austen, of Thackeray, of George Eliot, of Fielding? Is there anything in our experience answering to the episodes of the Lotus-Eaters, Calypso's Isle, the Cyclops' Cavern, the descent of the Goddess? Is the "reflection" even a reflection of Homer's own experience? Had he escaped from the cave under the belly of a ram? Had he been in the world of one-eyed giants? Were his friends in the habit of talking in hexameter verse? We may go on, of course, but is it worth while? It is surely hardly necessary to demonstrate the fact that the author of the "Morte D'Arthur" had never seen the Graal, that such a character as Don Quixote never existed in the natural order of things. We might have gone more sharply to work with this "fidelity" test: we might have said that poetry being, admittedly fine literature at its finest, and (admittedly also) being unfaithful to life as we know it both in matter and manner, that therefore the test breaks down at once. If fine literature must be faithful to life, then "Kubla Khan" is not fine literature; which, I think we may say, is highly absurd.

I daresay you think I have dealt rather crudely, in a somewhat materialistic spirit, with this criterion of "fidelity to life." I admit the charge, but you must remember that I am dealing with very bad people, who understand nothing but materialism. And when these people tell you in so many words that it is the author's business clearly and intelligently to present the life—the common, social life around him—then, believe me, the only thing to be done is to throw

"Odyssey" and "Œdipus," "Morte D'Arthur," "Kubla Khan" and "Don Quixote" straight in their faces, and to demonstrate that these eternal books were not constructed on the proposed receipt. Of course if I were treating with the initiated, if I were commentating and not arguing, I should handle the great masterpieces in a much more reverent manner. I mean that for those who possess the secret it skills not to bring in the Cyclops (who for us is not a giant but a symbol); we have only to bow down before the great music of such a poem as the Odyssey, recognising that by the very reason of its transcendent beauty, by the very fact that it trespasses far beyond the world of our daily lives, beyond "selection" and "reflection," it is also exalted above our understanding, that because its beauty is supreme, that therefore its beauty is largely beyond criticism. For ourselves we do not need to prove its transcendence of life by this or that extraordinary incident; it is the whole spirit and essence and sound and colour of the song that affect us; and we know that the Odyssey surpassed the bounds of its own age and its own land just as much as it surpasses those of our time and our country. You look as if you thought I were fighting with the vanquished, but let me tell you that great people have praised Homer because he depicted truthfully the men and manners of his time.

But as I was saying, all this would be too subtle for the enemy, for the people who maintain that fine literature is a faithful reflection of life, and think that Jane Austen touched the point of literary supremacy. With them, as I said, we must be rough; we must ask: Did Sophocles describe the ordinary life of Athens in his day? No: very well, then; since the works of Sophocles are fine literature, it follows that some fine literature does not reflect ordinary life, and therefore that fidelity to nature is not the differentia of the highest art.

I wonder whether I ought to caution you again against the ambiguity of language? We are dealing easily enough with such words as "life" and "nature," and from what you know of my system you may perhaps have seen that I have been using these words as the people use them, as those use them who would say that "Vanity Fair" is a faithful presentation of life. I thought you would understand this, but I may just mention in passing that words like "nature," "life" and "truth" or "fidelity" have also their esoteric values, that (by way of example) the truth of the scientist and the truth of the philosopher are two very different things. So it may turn out by and bye that in the occult sense, "fidelity to life" is the differentia of fine literature; that the aim of art is truth; that the artist continually mirrors nature in its eternal, essential forms; but for the present moment, it is understood, is it not, that these words have been used in their common, everyday popular significance? The "Dunciad" is a study of man, and Wordsworth's "Ode on Intimations of Immortality" is a study of man, and the literary standpoint that we have been attacking is that of Pope and not that of Wordsworth.

If I remember, the next test we have to analyse is that of artifice, often and improperly called art. But I think we have already demolished this criterion. In distinguishing between art and artifice I pointed out that the latter merely signifies the adaptation of means to an end, and has no relation whatever with art properly so-called; it is simply the mental instrument with which man performs every task and every work of his daily life; it consists in the rejection of that which is unfit for the particular purpose in view, and in the acceptance and use of that which is fit for the desired end and likely to bring it about. It concerns not creation but execution, and it is I need hardly say as indispensable to the author as are his pen and ink, and (I might almost say) is as little concerned as these with the essence of his art. Of course in works of the very highest genius we may declare that, in a sense, art has become all in all, that the necessary artifice has been interpenetrated with art, so that we can hardly distinguish in our minds between the idea and the realisation of it. In such cases, artifice has been lifted up and exalted into the heaven of art, and it remains artifice no longer; but in the view that we are considering it is merely the adaptation of means to an end, a clever choice of incident, the knack of putting in and leaving out. The faculty may, as I said, be glorified and transfigured by genius, but every newspaper reporter must have more or less of it, and it is clear enough I think (perhaps I may mention Wilkie Collins once more) that in itself it cannot establish the claim of any book to be fine literature.

And lastly we have to deal with style; and here again I must have recourse to my distinctions. What is a good style? If you mean by a "good" style, one that delivers the author's meaning in the clearest possible manner, if its purpose and effect are obviously utilitarian, if it be designed solely with the view of imparting knowledge—the knowledge of what the author intends—then I must point out that "style" in this sense is or should be amongst the accomplishments of every commercial clerk—indeed, it will be merely a synonym for plain speaking and plain writing—and in this sense it is evidently not one of the marks of art, since the object of art is not information, but a peculiar kind of æsthetic delight. But if on the other hand style is to mean such a use and choice of words and phrases and cadences that the ear and the soul through the ear receive an impression of subtle but most beautiful music, if the sense and sound and colour of the words affect us with an almost inexplicable delight, then I say that while Idea is the soul, style is the glorified body of the very highest literary art. Style, in short, is the last perfection of the very best in literature, it is the outward sign of the burning grace within. But we must keep the systematic consideration of style for some other night; it's not a subject to be dealt with by the way, and I have only said so much because it was necessary to draw the line between language as a means of imparting facts (good style in the sense of our opponents) and language as an æsthetic instrument, which is a good, or rather a beautiful style in our sense. In the latter sense it is the form of fine literature, in the former sense it is the medium of all else that is expressed in words, from a bill of exchange upwards.

It seems to me, then, that we have considered one by one the alternative tests of fine literature which have been or may be proposed, and we have come to the conclusion that each and all are impossible. It is no longer permissible, I imagine, for you or for me to say: "This book is fine literature because it makes me cry, because it was so interesting that I couldn't put it down, because it is so natural and faithful to life, because it is so well (plainly and neatly) written." We have picked these reasons to pieces one by one, and the result is that we are driven back on my "word of the enigma"— Ecstasy; the infallible instrument, as I think, by which fine literature may be discerned from reading-matter, by which art may be known from artifice, and style from intelligent expression. At any rate we have got our hypothesis, and you remember what stress Coleridge laid on the necessity of forming some hypothesis before entering on any investigation.

I believe we began to-night with the evening paper, and the strange glimpse it gives us, through a pinky-green veil, through a cloud of laborious nonsense about odds and winners and tips and all such foolery, into that ancient eternal desire of man for the unknown.

And that, you remember, was one of the synonyms that I offered you for ecstasy; and so in a sense I expect that we shall have the evening paper close beside us all the way of our long voyage in quest of the lost Atlantis.

II

I think it is a horrible thing to have such a good memory as that. I recollect, now that you remind me, that I did lay down "Pickwick" v. "Vanity Fair" as a sort of test case of my theory of literature; but you surely do not expect me to work out the arguments in detail? Of course if I were giving a series of lectures I should "set a paper" after each one; but I expect you to content yourself with the suggestion, with the skeleton map, as it were. Besides, if we take that special case of two eminent Victorian novels as a concrete instance of the abstract argument, don't you see that we are answering the particular question all the while that we are investigating the general proposition? Surely if you recollect all that we said about fine literature in general, you won't have much difficulty in adjudicating on the claims of Thackeray. Don't you see that he never withdraws himself from the common life and the common consciousness, that he is all the while nothing but a photographer; a showman with a set of pictures. A consummately clever photographer, certainly, a showman with a gift of amusing, interesting "patter" that is quite extraordinary, an artificer of very high merit. But where will you find Ecstasy in Thackeray? Where is his adoration? You may search, I think, from one end of his books to the other, without finding any evidence that he realised the mystery of things; he was never for a moment aware of that shadowy double, that strange companion of man, who walks, as I said, foot to foot with each one of us, and yet his paces are in an unknown world. And (unless you have got any fresh arguments) I think we decided last week that the book which lacks the sense of all this is not fine literature.

I hope you don't think I am abusing Thackeray. I am always

reading him, and I chose his "Vanity Fair" because it strikes me as such a supremely clever example of its class. I suppose there is nothing more amusing than the society of a brilliant, observant man of the world. Well, Thackeray was brilliant and observant in excelsis, and besides that, he understood the artifice of story-telling, and he could write a terse, clean-cut English which was always sufficient for his purpose. He contrives the corporal overthrow of the Marquis of Steyne, he shows you that bald old nobleman sprawling on the floor, and the words that he uses are his brisk, willing, and capable servants. He has observation, and artifice, and "style" in that secondary sense which we distinguished from the real style; from those "melodies unheard" which I called (I think rather picturesquely) the glorified body of the highest literary art. But these qualities, we found out, are not, separately or conjointly, the differentia of fine literature as we understand the term; and consequently, with all our admiration and all our interest we are compelled to place Thackeray in the lower form, simply because he is clearly and decisively lacking in that one essential quality of ecstasy, because he never leaves the street and the highroad to wander on the eternal hills, because he does not seem to be aware that such hills exist.

Of course I have only taken Thackeray as the representative of his class, and I chose him, as I remarked, because, for me, he is the most favourable representative of it. I am thinking, really, of the "plain man" whom we have engaged in so many forms, and of his "plain" argument which comes to this—"for me a great book is a book that amuses me greatly and that I enjoy reading." And I say that Thackeray amuses me greatly and that I enjoy reading his books immensely, but that, with due respect to "common sense," such an argument fails to prove that "Vanity Fair" is fine literature.

Other people would, no doubt, have chosen other books; many would have selected Miss Austen, and I daresay they would have a good deal to say for their choice. Undoubtedly there is a severity, a self-restraint, a fineness of observation, a delicacy of irony in "Pride and Prejudice" which are unmatched of their kind (the Thackeray of the caricatures, of those queer woodblocks, comes out now and then in the books, and digression occasionally goes beyond due bounds); but I named "Vanity Fair" because, personally, I find it more amusing than "Pride and Prejudice." In neither of these books is there art in our high sense of the word, and in preferring the one over the other I am simply saying that I prefer the company of a brilliant and witty cosmopolitan to that of a very keen and delicate, but very limited maiden lady, who lives in a remote country town and understands thoroughly the reason why the vicar bowed so low when a certain carriage rolled up the high street, and why that pretty, prim girl crossed over the way when the handsome gentleman from the Hall came out of the chymist's. Yes, the cosmopolitan at the club window certainly fails a little in his manners now and then, and the country gentlewoman's breeding is perfect of its kind, but the circles in which Pendennis moved are (to me) so infinitely the more entertaining of the two.

You see, I think that the question of liking a book or not liking it has nothing whatever to do with the consideration of fine art. Art is there, if I may say so, just as the Tenth Commandment is there; and if we don't like them, so much the worse for us. I may find Homer very dull reading, I may covet your ox and your ass and everything that is yours, but my limited and somewhat commonplace brains, and my envy of your prosperity won't alter the fact that the "Odyssey" is fine literature and that covetousness is wicked. But when we once leave the utterances of the eternal, universal human ecstasy, which we have agreed to call art, and descend to these lower levels that we are talking of now, it seems to me that the question of liking or not liking counts for a good deal. Not for everything, of course. We must still distinguish: between plots stupid or ingenious, between observation that is close and keen and observation that is vague and inaccurate, between artifice and the want of it, between sentences that are neatly constructed and mere slipshod. All these things naturally reckon in the account, but when they have been estimated and allowed their value, you will usually find that you are influenced still more by your mere liking or disliking of the subject-matter, and it seems to me quite legitimately. For, if you look closely into the whole question, you will find that you are judging these secondary books as you judge of life, as you choose the scene of your holiday, as you read the newspaper. One man may say that he prefers to talk to artists, another, quite legitimately, may love the society of brewers; you may think Norway perfection, I am going to Constantinople; A. turns at once to the quotation for Turpentine at Savannah, B. folds down the sheet at the Police News. It is not a question of art, but of taste, that is of individual humour and constitution; you frequent the company that suits you, you go to the place you like, you read the news that happens to be most interesting from your special standpoint. And in the same way, if I find the conversation of Miss Becky Sharpe, as reported by Mr W. M. Thackeray, more amusing than the conversation of Miss Elizabeth Bennett as reported by Miss Jane Austen; it seems to me that there is no more to be said. Elizabeth's remarks are more skilfully reported? Very likely, but, granting that, I had rather listen to the record, imperfect, if you please, of the other lady's conversation. Here is a speech on Bimetallism, given at great length, and (let us presume) with great accuracy; here is a short summary of Professor L.'s "Lecture on the Eleusinian Mysteries," very badly "sub-edited." But, you see, I happen not to care twopence about Bimetallism, so I turn away from the careful report, growling; while I cut out that wretched summary of the Lecture with the purpose of pasting it in my scrap-book, since every word about the Eleusinian Mysteries has a vivid interest for me.

It often amuses me to hear people quarrelling about the rival "artistic merit" of books which have, in most cases, no artistic merits at all. A. writes a book about greengrocers, and you, who find something singularly piquant and entertaining in the manners, speech, and habits of the class in question, pronounce A. to be a "great artist" who has written a masterpiece. I love dukes, and B's. novel of the peerage strikes me as a marvel of artistic accomplishment, while I pronounce the work that has charmed you to be as stupid and tiresome as the class it represents. Each of us is talking nonsense; there is no art in the question, which is purely a matter of individual taste. The Stock Exchange column interests one man, while the latest football news absorbs the other. That is all.

Of course, as I said, artifice counts for something: there is a pleasure in seeing the thing neatly done, and I suppose it is this pleasure that has secured Miss Austen her fervent admirers. It is a little difficult to treat this form of pleasure quite fairly; a musician perhaps would find it difficult to answer the question whether he would rather hear Palestrina badly rendered or Zingarelli executed to perfection. In the latter case there would certainly be the charm of exquisite voices in perfect order and accord, though the music were nothing or worse than nothing; still, our musician might say, on the other hand, that Palestrina martyred was better than Zingarelli triumphant. I am afraid I can imagine myself saying: "Limited

31

country-people, as seen by Jane Austen, are so 'slow' that they rather bore me, though the author has portrayed them with wonderful skill," but I can hardly fancy myself affirming that Becky Sharpe is such an interesting personage that she would still delight me, even if the author of "Ten Thousand a Year" had written her history. On the other hand I believe that the plot of "Jekyll and Hyde" would still have had some fascination, though it had been treated by the veriest dolt in letters. But that is not a good example, since "Jekyll and Hyde" is certainly in its conception, though not in its execution, a work of fine art. Let us take the "Moonstone" again as an example; I believe then, that if the events related in it had caught our eyes in a brief newspaper paragraph they would still have interested.

It seems to me that, after all, this question of artifice, of "how the thing is done," comes under the same category as liking and disliking. I mean it is largely a matter of the personal equation, about which no very strict laws can be laid down. You might say, for example, that Becky would entertain you in any hands, however indifferent, provided that her "facts" were preserved, and I don't see that I could argue the point with you. It reminds me again of the way in which men choose their friends; one lays stress on pleasant manners, another on sterling goodness of character, a third on wit, a fourth on distinction of some kind; and argument is really voiceless. "Here is a book-case," you may say, "look how exquisitely it is made." Yes, but I don't want a book-case; whereas that table, ricketty as it is, will be really useful. But if you were to say: "Look at Westminster Abbey," you can hardly imagine my answering: "Bother Westminster Abbey; I want a pig-sty." You see how, here again, we come to the generic difference between fine literature and interesting reading matter. We read the "Odyssey" because we are supernatural, because we hear in it the echoes of the eternal song, because it symbolises for us certain amazing and beautiful things, because it is music; we read Miss Austen and Thackeray because we like to recognise the faces of our friends aptly reproduced, to see the external face of humanity so deftly mimicked, because we are natural. The question of our preference for one over the other, is, making due allowance for analogy, the question of our preference for a table over a bookcase or vice versâ, and the workmanship in each case is largely a matter of detail. And the great poem may be equated with the great church: each is made for beauty, the one is ecstasy in words, the other ecstasy in stone. But the church and the pig-sty, on the other hand, are not to be compared together: incidentally, no doubt, the former is rainproof or in ill repair, has good or bad acoustic properties, while the latter may be either an æsthetic pest in the back-yard, or an agreeable looking little shed enough. Still, the essence of the church is beauty, ecstasy; of the sty utility, the safe keeping of pigs. It would be absurd, you see, to say: "I prefer an abbey to a pig-sty," and it would be equally absurd to say: "I prefer the 'Œdipus' to 'Pride and Prejudice'" or "I prefer the Venus of the Louvre to the wax-figures in the exhibition." Of course these are only analogies, and you mustn't press them, but they may help to make my meaning clearer, to enforce the vast distinction between art and artifice. Please don't think that I wish to establish a proportion: as a pig-sty is to an abbey, so is Jane Austen to Sophocles. In her case you would have to substitute a neat Georgian house for "pig-sty" and then I think you would have a very fair proportion. But all that I wanted to do was to draw the line between things made for use, to occupy some definite place in relation to our common daily life; and things made by ecstasy and for ecstasy, things that are symbols, proclaiming the presence of the unknown world.

And I chose "Pickwick" as the antithesis to "Vanity Fair" deliberately. Thackeray (in my private judgment) is the chief of those who have provided interesting reading-matter; Dickens is by no means in the first rank of literary artists. I think he is golden, but he is very largely alloyed with baser stuff, with indifferent metal, which was the product of his age, of his circumstances in life, of his own uncertain taste. Just contrast the atmosphere which surrounded the young Sophocles, with that in which the young Dickens flourished. Both were men of genius, but one grew up in the City of the Violet Crown, the other in Camden Town and worse places, one was accustomed to breathe that "most pellucid air," the other inhaled the "London particular." The wonder is, not that there are faults in Dickens, but that there is genius of any kind. I am not going to analyze "Pickwick" any more than I analyzed "Vanity Fair," but of course you see that, in its conception, it is essentially one with the "Odyssey." It is a book of wandering; you start from your own doorstep and you stray into the unknown; every turn of the road fills you with surmise, every little village is a discovery, a something new, a creation. You know not what may happen next; you are journeying through another world. I need not remind you how glorious all this is in the Odyssey, which of course is so much more beautiful than "Pickwick," as that glowing Mediterranean Sea, whose bounds on every side were mystery, is more beautiful than the muddy, foggy Thames, as those rolling hexameters are more beautiful than Dickens's prose; and yet in each case the symbol is, in reality, the same; both the heroic song of the old Ionian world and the comic cockney romance of 1837 communicate that enthralling impression of the unknown, which is, at once, a whole philosophy of life, and the most exquisite of emotions. In varying degrees of intensity you will trace it all through fine literature in every age and in every nation; you will find it in Celtic voyages, in the Eastern

Tale, where a door in a dull street suddenly opens into dreamland, in the mediæval stories of the wandering knights, in "Don Quixote," and at last in our "Pickwick" where Ulysses has become a retired city man, whimsically journeying up and down the England of sixty years ago. You talk of the "grotesquerie" of "Pickwick," but don't you see that this element is present in all the masterpieces of the kind? Remember the Cyclops, remember the grotesque shapes that decorate the "Arabian Nights," remember the bizarre element, the almost wanton grotesquerie of many of the "Arthur" romances. In all these cases as in "Pickwick" the same result is obtained; an overpowering impression of "strangeness," of remoteness, of withdrawal from the common ways of life. "Pickwick," is, in no sense, or in no valuable sense, a portrayal, a copy, an imitation of life in the ordinary sense of "imitation," and "life"; Pickwick, and Sam, and Jingle, and the rest of them are not clever reproductions of actual people, (is there any more foolish pursuit than that of disputing about the "original" of Mr Pickwick?); the book is rather the suggestion of another life, beneath our own or beside our own, and the characters, those queer grotesque people, are queer for the same reason that the Cyclops is queer and the dwarfs and dragons of mediæval romance are queer. We are withdrawn from the common ways of life; and in that withdrawal is the beginning of ecstasy. There are sentences in "Pickwick" that give me an almost extravagant delight. You remember the lines about the Lotus-Eaters.

> τῶν δ' ὅστις λωτοῖο φάγοι μελιηδέα καρπόν,
> οὐκέτ' ἀπαγγεῖλαι πάλιν ἤθελεν οὐδὲ νέεσθαι
> ἀλλ' αὐτοῦ βούλοντο μετ' ἀνδράσι Λωτοφάγοισιν
> λωτὸν ἐρεπτόμενοι μενέμεν νόστου τε λαθέσθαι.

Well, do you know there is a brief dialogue in "Pickwick" that seems almost as enchanted, to me. The scene is the manor-farm kitchen, on Christmas eve.

"'How it snows,' said one of the men, in a low voice.

"'Snows, does it?' said Wardle.

"'Rough, cold night, sir,' replied the man, 'and there's a wind got up that drifts it across the fields, in a thick white cloud.'

"'What does Jem say?' inquired the old lady. 'There ain't anything the matter, is there?'

"'No, no, mother,' replied Wardle; 'he says there's a snow-drift, and a wind that's piercing cold.'"

You know this is the introduction to the Tale of Gabriel Grub, an admirable legend which Dickens "farsed" with an obtrusive moral. But I confess that the atmosphere (which to me seems all the wild weather and the wild legend of the north) suggested by those phrases "a thick white cloud," and "a wind that's piercing cold" is in my judgment wholly marvellous. But Dickens, of course, is full of impressions which never become expressions. You remember that chapter about the lawyer's clerks in the "Magpie and Stump"? It is always quite pathetic to me to note how Dickens felt the strangeness, the mystery, the haunting that are like a mist about the old Inns of Court, and how utterly unable he was to express his emotion—to find a fit symbol for his meaning. He takes refuge, as it were, behind Jack Bamber, who tells two very insignificant legends as to the mystery of the Inns. Dickens feels that these legends are insignificant, and throws in one that is pure burlesque, and then changes the subject in despair; the vague impression has refused to be put into words; probably, indeed, it had stopped short of becoming thought. But I am afraid that if I once begin to talk about the defects and faults of Dickens I shall run on for ever, and I think you will be able to find out his laches quite well for yourself. What I want to insist on is his sense of mystery, his withdrawal from common life, and, finally, his ecstasy. I have not proved my case up to the hilt by a thorough-going analysis of "Pickwick," but I think I have suggested the "heads" of such an analysis. There is ecstasy in the main idea, in the thought of the man who wanders away from his familiar streets into unknown tracks and lanes and villages, there is ecstasy in the conception of all those queer, grotesque characters, reminders each one of the strangeness of life, there is ecstasy in the thought of the wild Christmas Eve, of the fields and woods scourged by "a wind that's piercing cold," hidden by the thick cloud of snow, there is ecstasy in that vague impression of the old, dark, Inns, of the "rotten" chambers that had been shut up for years and years. In a word: "Pickwick" is fine literature.

Well, you've got what you wanted; some sort of analysis of my case: "'Pickwick' v. 'Vanity Fair'"; but it must be clearly understood that I'm not going to "work out" every example. However, I am not sorry that I have been led to go into this particular case rather fully, because it is a typical one, and we shall not be obliged to go over the same ground again. I mean, that having witnessed the dissection of Thackeray, you will have no need to come to me for my judgment of George Eliot, or of Anthony Trollope, or—to make a very long list a very short one—of about ninety-nine per cent of our modern novels. Yes, you have mentioned a great name, and I, like you, take off my cap to the man who has gone on his way, without caring for the "public," or the "reviewers," or anything else, except his own judgment of what is right. But, frankly, if you pass from the man and come to his work, my plain opinion is this: that he has written about ordinary life, regarded from an ordinary standpoint, in a style which is extraordinary certainly, but very far from beautiful. It is not a beautiful style, since a fine style, though it may carry suggestion beyond the bourne of thought, though it may be the veil and visible body of concealed mysteries, is always plain on the surface. It may be like an ingeniously devised cryptogram, which may have an occult sense conveyed to initiated eyes in every dot and line and flourish, but is outwardly as simple and straightforward as a business letter. But in the works of the writer whom we are discussing obscurities, dubieties of all kinds are far from uncommon; and in many of his books there are passages which hardly seem to be English at all. The words are familiar— most of them—the grammatical construction often offers no very considerable difficulties—it is rarely, I mean, that one has to search very long for the nominative of the sentence—but when one has read the words and parsed them, one feels inclined to think that after all the passage is not in English but in some other language with a superficial resemblance to English. Style is not everything? Certainly not; a book may fail in style, and yet be fine, though not the finest literature. You have only to open Sir Walter Scott to have highly conclusive evidence on that point. But the writer we are considering not only fails in the body of art but even more conspicuously in the soul of it. Just think for a moment of his story of the very earnest Jew who fell in love with the baroness who was not very earnest. There was a false female friend, you remember, and social complications perturbed the hearts of the curiously assorted lovers, and finally the Jew was shot in a duel by another, less "detrimental," courtier. Can you conceive anything more trivial than this? Don't you see that from such a book as that the idea, the soul of fine literature, is completely lacking? Great books may always be summed up in a phrase, often in a single word, and that phrase or that word will always signify some primary and palmary idea. To me the only "idea" suggested by the plot I have outlined is unimportance; and, as in the case of Thackeray, ecstasy is entirely absent both from this and from all other of the author's books. You say that, after all, the plot in question is a plot of the love of a man for a woman, and that that is an idea in the highest sense of the word, and an idea which is the most of all fit for the purpose and the making of the finest literature. I agree with you in the latter clause of your sentence, but I must point out that the book is not the story of the love of a man for a woman, it is the story of the flirtation of a baroness with a German Jew Socialist—a very different matter. In a word, it is a tale of the accidental, of the particular, of the inessential; it is completely the play of Hamlet with the part of Hamlet omitted, and the greatest stress laid on the minor characters.

It is quite true that when an author writes a romance containing a hero and a heroine he must tell you who they are, he must give, briefly and succinctly, the necessary details—names, ages, conditions and so forth—but if he is a great author he will do this incidentally and make us feel that such details are incidental. In short, he must poise his feet on earth, but his way is to the stars. Think of the "Scarlet Letter," open it again and see how admirably Hawthorne has omitted a world of unessential details that a lesser man would have put in. He has left out a whole encyclopædia of useless and tedious information; there is the dim, necessary background of time and place, but in reality the scene is Eternity, and the drama is the Mystery of Love and Vengeance and Hell-fire. Of course fine literature must have its gross and carnal body, we must know "who's who," for I don't think an old-fashioned receipt that I remember was ever very successful. Oh, you must have read some of the tales I mean; they used to flourish in the old "Keepsakes," and the hero was boldly labelled "Fernando" for all distinction and description. One might surmise that Fernando was domiciled on the continent of Europe, but that was all. It was not successful, this well-meaning school of fiction, and I repeat that the finest literature must have its accidents—it cannot exist as shining substance alone. It is just the same with the art of sculpture, with the art of painting. You cannot look at a Greek Apollo without looking at that part of the body which conceals the bowels, but I imagine you don't want to treasure this thought or to insist on it? And I suppose a geologist, looking at a picture, could tell you whether those wild and terrible rocks were volcanic or carboniferous; but really one doesn't want to know. Bowels, geological formation, in sculpture and painting, the social position of the characters and all other such details in fine literature are inessential; and the great artist will, as I said, make us feel that they are inessential. If you want an instance of what I mean read a book which is very comparable with the German-Jew-Baroness tale that we were talking about. I mean "Two on a Tower" by Mr Hardy. In that you have the contrast of social ranks: the "two" are the Lady of the Manor and an educated peasant, but how utterly all thought of "society" (in any sense of the word) disappears from those wonderful pages, as you advance and find that the theme is really Love. Why even the accidents are glorified and are made of the essence of the book. The old tower standing in the midst of lonely, red ploughlands far from the highway, is at first only the convenient place where the young peasant studies astronomy; but as you read you feel the change coming, the tower is transmuted, glorified; every stone of it is aglow with mystic light; it is made the abode of the Lover and the Beloved, it is seen to be a symbol of Love, of an ecstasy, remote, and passionate, and eternal, dwelling far from the ways of men. Compare these two books, I say again, and you will know the chief distinction between fine literature and reading matter. To me, I confess, the "Jew-book" has not even interest of the lower sort, not by any means the interest of Thackeray, or Jane Austen or even of poor, dreary, draggle-tailed George Eliot; but if you are amused by it, I have no objection to make. You may be amused by the plates of the "Spring and Summer Novelties" in the lady's paper, if you please; but for heaven's sake don't come here and tell me that on the whole you prefer Botticelli's Primavera! Nay, but the fashion-plates are sometimes very nicely done, and they put in backgrounds, and they are trying to give the faces some character. Do get it into your head—firmly and fixedly—that the camera and the soul of man are two entirely different things.

You think the "photographic" comparison unfair, in this and other instances, because of the mechanical element in photography, because of that camera I have just mentioned? Well, I suppose that it is a little misleading. The sun and the camera between them certainly do your picture for you, and as you urge, there is more of artifice in the merest Sunday-school tale than in the best of photographs. Still, you must remember that photography too has its artifice, its choice of the right and the wrong way, and its exercise of judgment; there is a great deal in it that is not mechanical; and in its essence it is of the same class as the books I have been alluding to. The means employed are different, and a higher and finer artifice is required for making books than for taking photographs, but the end of each is the same, and that end is to portray the surface of life, to make a picture of the outside of things. It is on this ground that I defend my use of the analogy, and you must understand me to speak only of the object which is common to each, when I compare the secondary writer to a photographer. The writers, to be sure, have invention in a greater or less degree, but you will remark that the artists in literature have the power of creation, a totally different process. Invention is the finding of a thing in its more or less obscure hiding-place; creation is the making of a new thing, the invocation of Something from Nothingness. Don Quixote is a creation; the clergyman in "Pride and Prejudice" is an invention, Colonel Newcome is, in all probability, a composite portrait, while the Jew-Socialist who fell in love with the Baroness is simply a portrait of Ferdinand Lassalle.

You must remember that while the two classes—fine literature and reading matter—differ the one from the other generically, the individuals of each class differ from each other only specifically. Thus the difference in merit between the "Odyssey" and "Pickwick" is enormous, but it is a specific difference. In the same way it is hard to measure with the imagination the difference between "Madame Bovary" and that famous Sunday-school story "Jackie's Holiday": the former is immensely clever, the latter is immensely silly; but the two are, emphatically, of the same genus. In each case the effort of the author is to "describe life," the aim of Flaubert is absolutely identical with the aim of Miss Flopkins, and their results differ only as the Frenchman differs from the Englishwoman, the one being a serious and patient artificer while the other is a bungling idiot, who obtrudes her very empty personality and her very trashy ethics instead of studiously concealing them. Still: a photograph taken in the most famous studio in London is still a photograph equally with the spotted and misty effort of the amateur, and no amount of "touching-up" or "finishing," however patient it may be, will turn a photograph into a work of art. And, in like manner, no labour, no care, no polishing of the phrase, no patience in investigation, no artifice in plot or in construction will ever make "reading-matter" into fine literature.

III

I see that I shall be obliged to keep on reiterating the difference between fine literature and "literature," or in other words between art and observation expressed with artifice. I am afraid, that in your heart of hearts, you still believe that the "Odyssey" is fine literature, and that "Pride and Prejudice" is fine literature, though the "Odyssey" is "better" than "Pride and Prejudice." It is that "better" that I want to get out of your head, that monstrous fallacy of comparing Westminster Abbey with the charming old houses in Queen Square. You would see the absurdity of imagining that there can be any degree of comparison between two things entirely different, if I substituted for "Pride and Prejudice" some ordinary circulating-library novel of our own times. At least I hope you would see, though, as I told you a few weeks ago, I doubt very much whether many people realise the distinction between the "Odyssey" and a political pamphlet. The general opinion, I expect, is that both belong to the same class, though the Greek poem is much more "important" than the pamphlet. I think we succeeded in demonstrating the falsity of this idea, in showing clearly and decisively that fine literature means the expression of the eternal human ecstasy in the medium of words, and that it means nothing else whatsoever. Words, it is true, are used for other ends than this: they are used in sending telegrams to stockbrokers, for example, but why should this double office create any confusion? A tub and a tabernacle may each be made of wood, but you don't mix the two things up on that account? The other day you gave me a most amusing account of your landlady's quarrels with her servant girls. I remember that I laughed consumedly, and at the moment, that solemn preconisation of the servant Mabel to the effect that her mistress, Mrs Stickings, was not a "lydy," was more to my taste than the recitation of the "Ode on a Grecian Urn." But you surely didn't think that you were making literature all the while? Or that the history of Mrs Stickings and Mabel would have mysteriously become literature if you had written it down and got somebody to print it? Or that it would have been literature if some of the details had been a little exaggerated (I thought you had embroidered here and there); or if you had made the whole story up out of your own head? Exactly, you were, as you say, amusing me by the relation of facts a little altered, compressed, and embellished, and I am glad that you see that no process of writing or printing, no variation in the proportion of truth and invention, even to the total lack of all truth, could have changed an amusing presentation of the Stickings ménage into fine literature. But, surely, it is so very obvious. Did any cook ever think that he could change a turkey into a bird of paradise by careful attention to the farse and the sauce? The farmer might as well expect to breed early phœnixes for Leadenhall Market by the simple process of lighting a bonfire in the farmyard. The young ducks would jump into the blaze, and the transformation would be the work of a second! There is no more madness in that notion than in the other one—that one has only to print an amusing, interesting, life-like, or pathetic tale to make it into fine literature.

Yes; but what I am afraid is still lurking somewhere in your skull is this: that if only the stuffing is extremely well made, if only the sauce is an exquisite concoction, the turkey is, somehow or other, changed into a bird of paradise. That is, to translate the analogy, if only the plot is very ingenious, if only the construction is well carried out, if the characters are extremely life-like, if the English is admirably neat and sufficient, then reading-matter becomes fine literature. Make the bonfire high enough and your young ducks will be burned into phœnixes fast enough; let the artifice be sufficiently artificial and it will be art. Indeed you might as well maintain that a wooden statue, if it be really well carved, is thereby made into a gold statue.

Well, I remember saying one night that you were here that ecstasy is at once the most exquisite of emotions and a whole philosophy of life. And it is to the philosophy of life that we are brought, in the last resort. You know that there are, speaking very generally, two solutions of existence; one is the materialistic or rationalistic, the other, the spiritual or mystic. If the former were true, then Keats would be a queer kind of madman, and the "Morte d'Arthur" would be an elaborate symptom of insanity; if the latter is true, then "Pride and Prejudice" is not fine literature, and the works of George Eliot are the works of a superior insect—and nothing more. You must make your choice: is the story of the Graal lunacy, or not? You think it is not: then do not talk any more of turning glass into diamonds by careful polishing and cutting. Do not say: Mr A. spends five years over a book, and therefore what he writes is fine literature; Miss B. polishes off five novels in a year, and therefore she does not write fine literature. Do not say, Mr Shorthouse has got the name of a man who kept a private school in the time of Charles I. quite right; therefore "John Inglesant" is fine literature, while the archæological details in "Ivanhoe" are all wrong, therefore it is not fine literature. Good Lord! You might as well say: but my landlady's name is Mrs Stickings, and the girl (who left last month) was really called Mabel; therefore that story of mine was fine literature. What's that about sustained effort? Can you turn a deal ladder into a golden staircase by making it of a thousand rungs? What I say three times is right, eh? and if I tell the tale of Mrs

Stickings so that it extends to "our minimum length for three volume novels," it becomes fine literature.

Well, I really hope that we have at last settled the matter; that fine literature is simply the expression of the eternal things that are in man, that it is beauty clothed in words, that it is always ecstasy, that it always draws itself away, and goes apart into lonely places, far from the common course of life. Realise this, and you will never be misled into pronouncing mere reading-matter, however interesting, to be fine literature; and now that we clearly understand the difference between the two, I propose that we drop the "fine" and speak simply of literature.

But I assure you that, even after having established the grand distinction, it is by no means plain sailing. Everything terrestrial is so composite (except, perhaps, pure music) that one is confronted by an almost endless task of distinguishing matter from form, and body from spirit. Literature, we say, is ecstasy, but a book must be written about something and about somebody; it must be expressed in words, it must have arrangement and artifice, it must have accident as well as essence. Consider "Don Quixote" as an example; it is, I suppose, the finest prose romance in existence. Essentially, it expresses the eternal quest of the unknown, that longing, peculiar to man, which makes him reach out towards infinity; and he lifts up his eyes, and he strains his eyes, looking across the ocean, for certain fabled, happy islands, for Avalon that is beyond the setting of the sun. And he comes into life from the unknown world, from glorious places, and all his days he journeys through the world, spying about him, going on and ever on, expecting beyond every hill to find the holy city, seeing signs, and omens, and tokens by the way, reminded every hour of his everlasting citizenship. "From the great deep to the great deep he goes": it is true of King Arthur and

47

of each one of us; and this, I take it, is the essence of "Don Quixote," and of all his forerunners and successors. Then, in the second place, you get the eternal moral of the book, and you will understand that I am not using "moral" in the vulgar sense. The eternal moral, then, of "Don Quixote" is the strife between temporal and eternal, between the soul and the body, between things spiritual and things corporal, between ecstasy and the common life. You read the book and you see that there is a perpetual jar, you are continually confronted by the great antinomy of life. It seems a mere comic incident when the knight dreaming of enchantment is knocked about, and made ridiculous; but I tell you it is the perpetual tragedy of life itself, symbolised. I say that it is, under a figure, the picture of humanity in the world, that you will find the truth it represents repeated again and again throughout all history. You know that if one goes back resolutely to the first principles of things, one finds oneself, as it were, in a place where all lines that seemed parallel and eternally divided meet, and so it is with this tragedy symbolised by the Don Quixote. It is, you may say, the tragedy of the Unknown and the Known, of the Soul and Body, of the Idea and the Fact, of Ecstasy and Common Life; at last, I suppose, of Good and Evil. The source of it lies far beyond our understanding, but its symbol is shown again and again in Cervantes's page.

Then, there is a third element in the book. The author intended to write a burlesque on the current romances of chivalry; and he wrote, I suppose, the best burlesque that has ever been written, or ever will be written. If you unhappily so choose, you can shut your eyes to everything serious and everything beautiful, and read merely of Amadis and Arthur "taken off," of the highest ideals turned into nonsense, of the best motives shown to be, in effect, mischievous. You will read how the knight, in the approved manner of knights, helped the oppressed and the wretched, and how he usually worsened their condition tenfold. You may lend your ear to Sancho, grumbling and quoting "common-sense" proverbs all the road, as he rides on his ass, and if it were not for the wit and the comedy, you might fancy yourself in a suburban train bound for the city. Why, if you so please, "Don Quixote" is the Institute of cynicism, the reduction of every generous impulse to absurdity.

Finally, the knight is the mouthpiece of Cervantes himself, especially towards the end of the second part, where the armour and the fantasy drop off, piece by piece, and shred by shred, on that mournful, homeward journey. At last, I say, Don Quixote is almost simply Cervantes, commenting on men and affairs in Spain, and I think that in those final chapters the art has vanished together with the armour and the ecstasy. Yes, I always dread the ending of "Don Quixote." A star drops a line of streaming fire, down the vault of the sky, and perhaps you may have seen the ugly, shapeless thing that sinks into the earth.

But this very brief and imperfect analysis of a great masterpiece of literary art may give you some idea of the extraordinary complexity of all literature. As it is I have omitted one most important item in the account; I have said nothing of the style, because, I am sorry to say that I have no Spanish, and Cervantes speaks to me through an interpreter named Charles Jarvis. But, omitting style, you see that we have, in this particular case, five books in one; we have the utterance of pure ecstasy, the strife between ecstasy and the common life, the burlesque of chivalry, the institutes of cynicism, and the comments on affairs. Each of these different themes is managed with consummate ability, and (always excepting the last chapters of the book), each keeps its due place, so that it really rests with the reader, in a manner, to choose which book he is to read.

And then, there are other elements which must be accounted for if one is to judge a book as a whole, fairly and thoroughly. I may be so charmed with the writer's rapture, with the wonder and beauty of his idea, that I may forget the fact that the artist must also be the artificer; that while the soul conceives, the understanding must formulate the conception, that while ecstasy must suggest the conduct of the story, common-sense must help to range each circumstance in order, that while an inward, mysterious delight must dictate the burning phrases and sound in the music and melody of the words, cool judgment must go through every line, reminding the author that, if literature be the language of the Shadowy Companion it must yet be translated out of the unknown speech into the vulgar tongue. Here then we have the elements of a book. Firstly the Idea or Conception, the thing of exquisite beauty which dwells in the author's soul, not yet clothed in words, nor even in thought, but a pure emotion. Secondly, when this emotion has taken definite form, is made incarnate as it were, in the shape of a story, which can be roughly jotted down on paper, we may speak of the Plot. Thirdly, the plot has to be systematised, to be drawn to scale, to be carried out to its legitimate conclusions, to be displayed by means of Incident; and here we have Construction. Fourthly, the story is to be written down, and Style is the invention of beautiful words which shall affect the reader by their meaning, by their sound, by their mysterious suggestion.

This, then, is the fourfold work of literature, and if you want to be perfect you must be perfect in each part. Art must inspire and shape each and all, but only the first, the Idea, is pure art; with Plot, and Construction, and Style there is an alloy of artifice. If then any given book can be shown to proceed from an Idea, it is to be placed in the class of literature, in the shelf of the "Odyssey" as I think I once expressed it. It may be placed very high in the class; the more it have of rapture in its every part, the higher it will be: or, it may be placed very low, because, for example, having once admired the Conception, the dream that came to the author from the other world, we are forced to admit that the Story or Plot was feebly imagined, that the Construction was clumsily carried out, that the Style is, æsthetically, non-existent. You will notice that I am never afraid of blaming my favourites, of finding fault with the books which I most adore. I can do so freely and without fear of consequences, since having once applied my test, and having found that "Pickwick," for example, is literature, I am not in the least afraid that I shall be compelled to eat my words if flaws in plot and style and construction are afterwards made apparent. The statue is gold; we have settled that much, and we need not fear that it will turn into lead, if we find that the graving and carving is poor enough. Once be sure that your temple is a temple, and I will warrant you against it being suddenly transmuted into a tub, through the discovery of scamped workmanship.

Well, suppose we begin to apply our analysis. Let us take the strange case of Mr R. L. Stevenson, and especially his "Jekyll and Hyde," which, in some ways, is his most characteristic and most effective book. Now I suppose that instructed opinion (granting its existence) was about equally divided as to the class in which this most skilful and striking story was to be placed. Many, I have no doubt, gave it a very high place in the ranks of imaginative literature, or (as we should now say) in the ranks of literature; while many other judges set it down as an extremely clever piece of sensationalism, and nothing more. Well, I think both these opinions are wrong; and I should be inclined to say that "Jekyll and Hyde" just scrapes by the skin of its teeth, as it were, into the shelves of literature, and no more. On the surface it would seem to be merely sensationalism; I expect that when you read it, you did so with breathless absorption, hurrying over the pages in your eagerness to find out the secret, and this secret once discovered, I imagine that "Jekyll and Hyde" retired to your shelf—and stays there, rather dusty. You have never opened it again? Exactly. I have read it for a second time, and I was astonished to find how it had, if I may say so, evaporated. At the first reading one was enthralled by mere curiosity, but when once this curiosity had been satisfied what remained? If I may speak from my own experience, simply a rather languid admiration of the ingenuity of the plot with its construction, combined with a slight feeling of impatience, such as one might experience if one were asked to solve a puzzle for the second time. You see that the secret once disclosed, all the steps which lead to the disclosure become, ipso facto, insignificant, or rather they become nothing at all, since their only significance and their only existence lay in the secret, and when the secret has ceased to be a secret, the signs and cyphers of it fall also into the world of nonentity. You may be amazed, and perplexed, and entranced by a cryptogram, while you are solving it, but the solution once attained, your cryptogram is either nothing or perilously near to nothingness.

Well, all this points, doesn't it, towards mere sensationalism, very cleverly done? But, as I said, I think "Jekyll and Hyde" just scrapes over the border-line and takes its place, very low down, among books that are literature. And I base my verdict solely on the Idea, on the Conception that lies, buried rather deeply, beneath the Plot. The plot, in itself, strikes me as mechanical—this actual physical transformation, produced by a drug, linked certainly with a theory of ethical change, but not linked at all with the really mysterious, the really psychical—all this affects me, I say, as ingenious mechanism and nothing more; while I have shown how the construction is ingenious artifice, and the style is affected by the same plague of laboured ingenuity. Throughout it is a thoroughly conscious style, and in literature all the highest things are unconsciously, or at least, subconsciously produced. It has music, but it has no under-music, and there are no phrases in it that seem veils of dreams, echoes of the "inexpressive song." It is on the conception, then, alone, that I justify my inclusion of "Jekyll" amongst works of art; for it seems to me that, lurking behind the plot, we divine the presence of an Idea, of an inspiration. "Man is not truly one, but truly two," or, perhaps, a polity with many inhabitants, Dr Jekyll writes in his confession, and I think that I see here a trace that Mr Stevenson had received a vision of the mystery of human nature, compounded of the dust and of the stars, of a dim vast city, splendid and ruinous as drowned Atlantis deep beneath the waves, of a haunted quire where a flickering light burns before the Veil. This, I believe, was the vision that came to the artist, but the admirable artificer seized hold of it at once and made it all his own, omitting what he did not understand, translating roughly from the unknown tongue, materialising, coarsening, hardening. Don't you see how thoroughly physical the actual plot is, and if one escapes for a moment from the atmosphere of the laboratory it is only to be confronted by the most obvious vein of moral allegory; and from this latter light, "Jekyll and Hyde" seems almost the vivid metaphor of a clever preacher. You mustn't imagine, you know, that I condemn the powder business as bad in itself, for (let us revert for a moment to philosophy) man is a sacrament, soul manifested under the form of body, and art has to deal with each and both and to show their interaction and interdependence. The most perfect form of literature is, no doubt, lyrical poetry which is, one might say, almost pure Idea, art with scarcely an alloy of artifice, expressed in magic words, in the voice of music. In a word, a perfect lyric, such as Keats's "Belle Dame Sans Mercy" is almost pure soul, a spirit with the luminous body of melody. But (in our age, at all events) a prose romance must put on a grosser and more material envelope than this, it must have incident, corporeity, relation to material things, and all these will occupy a considerable part of the whole. To a certain extent, then, the Idea must be materialised, but still it must always shine through the fleshly vestment; the body must never be mere body but always the body of the spirit, existing to conceal and yet to manifest the spirit; and here it seems to me that Mr Stevenson's story breaks down. The transformation of Jekyll into Hyde is solely material, as you read it, without artistic significance; it is simply an astounding incident, and not an outward sign of an inward mystery. As for the possible allegory I have too much respect for Mr Stevenson as an artificer to think that he would regard this element as anything but a very grave defect. Allegory, as Poe so well observed, is always a literary vice, and we are only able to enjoy the "Pilgrim's Progress" by forgetting that the allegory exists. Yes, that seems to me the vitium of "Jekyll and Hyde": the conception has been badly realised, and by badly I do not mean clumsily, because from the logical, literal standpoint, the plot and the construction are marvels of cleverness; but I mean inartistically: ecstasy, which as we have settled is the synonym of art, gave birth to the idea, but immediately abandoned it to artifice, and to artifice only, instead of presiding over and inspiring every further step in plot, in construction, and in style. All this may seem to you very fine-drawn and over-subtle, but I am convinced that it is the true account of the matter, and perhaps you may realise my theory better if I draw out that analogy of "translation" which I suggested, I think, a few minutes ago. I was passing along New Oxford Street the other day, and I happened to look into a shop which displays Bibles in all languages, and I glanced at the French version, open at the seventh chapter of the Book of Proverbs. I saw the words "un jeune homme dépourvu de bon sens," and then, lower down, "comme un bœuf à la boucherie," and it was some considerable time before I realised that these phrases "translated," "a young man void of understanding," and "as an ox goeth to the slaughter." Now you notice that these are in every way commonplace examples; there is nothing extraordinarily poetical in either phrase as it stands in the Authorised Version. I might have made the contrast much more violent by choosing a passage from the Song of Songs or Ecclesiastes; and I wonder how "Therefore with Angels and Archangels" would go into French. But isn't the gulf astounding between "void of understanding" and "dépourvu de bon sens"? Yet the meaning of the French is really the same as the meaning of the English; logically, I should think, the two phrases are exactly equivalent. And yet ... well, we know perfectly well that "dépourvu de bon sens" in no way renders that noble and austere simplicity that we reverence in the English text.

Now, I think, you ought to see what I have been trying to express about the gulf that may open always between the conception and the plot, or story, that does divide the conception from the plot of "Jekyll and Hyde." Of course the analogy is not perfect, because the magnum chaos that yawns between the unformulated Idea and the formulated plot, between pure ecstasy and ecstasy plus artifice, is much vaster than the distinction between English and French, indeed between the two former there is almost or altogether the difference of the infinite and the finite, of soul and body; still, you see how a book is a rendering, a translation of an Idea, and how a very fine idea may be embodied in a very mechanical plot.

You remember the "Socialist and Baroness" novel that we were talking about the other night. We placed it outside of literature firstly and chiefly because it was not based on ecstasy, on an idea of any kind, and secondly, and by way of consequence, because in its execution and detail it was so thoroughly insignificant, because it played Hamlet with the part of the Prince omitted. Now I think that it is strong evidence of the soundness of my literary theory that we are enabled by it to take two books so utterly dissimilar in manner and method, in story and treatment, and to judge them both by the same scale. For this is what it really comes to: we say that the "Tragic Comedians" is not literature because it simply tells of facts without their significance, because it deals with the outward show and not with the inward spirit, because it is accidental and not essential. And in just the same way we say that "Jekyll and Hyde" (its conception apart) is not literature inasmuch as it too has the body of a story without the soul of a story, the incident, the fact, without the inward thing of which the fact is a symbol. For if you will consider the matter you will see that a fact qua fact has no existence in art at all. It is not the painter's business to make us a likeness of a tree or a rock; it is his business to communicate to us an emotion—an ecstasy, if you please—and that he may do so he uses a tree or a rock as a symbol, a word in his language of colour and form. It is not the business of the sculptor to chisel likenesses of men in marble; the human form is to him also a symbol which stands for an idea. In the same manner it is not the business of the literary artist to describe facts—real or imaginary—in words: he is possessed with an idea which he symbolises by incident, by a story of men and women and things. He is possessed, let us say, by the idea of Love: then he must write a story of lovers, but he must never forget that A. and B., his actual lovers in the tale, with their social positions, their whims and fancies, their sayings and doings are only of consequence in the degree that they symbolise the universal human passion, which in its turn is a copy of certain eternal and ineffable things. If A. and B. do not do this then they are nothing, and worse than nothing, so far as art is concerned. "But my tree is like a tree," says the dull painter, and "my anatomy is faultless," says the bad sculptor, and "my characters are life-like," says the novelist.

And one can apply exactly the same reasoning to Mr Stevenson's ingenious story. I do not know whether there is, or has been, or will be a salt in existence which can turn a man into another person; that is of not the slightest consequence to the argument. The result of the powder, as it is described in the book, is an incident, and it makes no difference to the critical judgment whether the incident is true or false, probable or improbable. The only point, absolutely the only point is this: is the incident significant or insignificant, is it related for its own sake, or is it posited because it is a sign, a symbol, a word which veils and reveals the artist's ecstasy and inspiration? The socialist fell in love with the baroness: it is true, you say, it really happened so in Germany some twenty-five years ago. But in the book it is insignificant. The doctor took the powder and became another man; it is probably untrue. But it is also insignificant; and to the critic of art in literature the one incident stands precisely on the same footing as the other.

And, do you know, I am glad I have made this comparison between "Jekyll and Hyde" and the "Tragic Comedians," because it has struck me that what I have been saying about the essential element of all literature might be open to very grave misunderstanding. I have been insisting, with reiteration that must have tired you, that there is only one test by which literature may be distinguished from mere reading matter, and that that test is summed up in the word, ecstasy. And then we admitted a whole string of synonyms—desire of the unknown, sense of the unknown, rapture, adoration, mystery, wonder, withdrawal from the common life—and I daresay I have used many other phrases in the same sense without giving you any special warning that it was our old friend again in a new guise. But it has just occurred to me that with all this wealth of synonyms, I may not have made my meaning perfectly clear. For example, while I was laying down the law about Dr Jekyll's powder and its effects, you might have interrupted me with the remark: "But I thought you said the sense of wonder was characteristic of literature; and surely the change from Jekyll into Hyde is extremely wonderful." Or again, when I was belauding the "Odyssey," dwelling on the voyage of Ulysses amongst strange peoples, you might have put in some modern tale of strange adventure, and requested me to distinguish between the two, to justify my praise of the old, and rejection of the new. And we have mentioned Sunday-school books, always, I think, with a certain nuance of contempt; but Sunday-school books usually deal with religion, and religion and adoration are almost synonymous. And so one could go on with the list, making out, on our premises, with our own test, a plausible case for books which we know very well are neither literature nor anything remotely approaching it. And that would look rather like the collapse of our literary case, wouldn't it?

Well, the solution of the difficulty seems to me to be sought for in the remarks I was making just now about "facts" in art. I said, you remember, that in art, facts as facts have no existence at all. Facts, incidents, plots, simply form the artistic speech—its mode of expression, or medium—and if there is no idea behind the facts, then you have no longer language but gibberish. Just as language is made up of the letters of the alphabet, arranged in significant words and sentences; so is the artistic language made up of plots, incidents, sentences which are informed with significance. If I heap up letters of the alphabet, and arrange them in an arbitrary collocation, without meaning, I am forming gibberish, and not a language; and so if I pepper my pages with extraordinary incidents, without attaching to them any significance, I am writing, it may be, an exciting, absorbing, interesting book, but I am not making literature. Indeed, some of the books that might be mentioned in this connection remind me of a man swearing: he uses the holiest names but he does so in such a manner that he excites not reverence and awe but disgust and repulsion. Tell the bare "plot" of the Odyssey to one of these writers, and hint that it might be made into a "successful Christmas book for boys," and he will produce you a book which will contain the Lotus-Eaters, and Calypso and the Cyclops, but which will have just the same relation to literature as blasphemy bears to the Liturgy. That seems to me the explanation; one must say again that mere incident is nothing, that it only becomes something when it is a symbol of an interior meaning. And, turning this maxim inside out, as it were, we shall sometimes find that a book which seems on the surface to be "reading matter" is really literature, and incidents, apparently insignificant, may turn out, on a closer examination, to be significant and symbolic in a very high degree. So I don't think our literary criterion is in any way invalidated by the occurrence of surprising incidents in very worthless books. Look at "Mr Isaacs" for example. In a sense it is a "wonderful" book, inasmuch as it contains incidents which are far removed from common experience; but you have only to read it to discover that the author had not been visited by any inspiration of the unseen. One may trace some acquaintance with theosophical "literature," but not even the dimmest vision of "the other things." The "other things"? Ah, that is another synonym, but who can furnish a precise definition of the indefinable? They are sometimes in the song of a bird, sometimes in the scent of a flower, sometimes in the whirl of a London street, sometimes hidden under a great lonely hill. Some of us seek them with most hope and the fullest assurance in the sacring of the Mass, others receive tidings through the sound of music, in the colour of a picture, in the shining form of a statue, in the meditation of eternal truth. Do you know that I can never hear a jangling piano-organ, contending with the roar of traffic without the tears—not of feeling but of emotion—coming to my eyes?

And that instance—it is grotesque enough—reminds me that I think I have an explanation of another puzzle that has often perplexed me, and I daresay has perplexed you. Do you remember the books that you read when you were a boy? I can think of stories that I read long ago (I have forgotten the very names of them) that filled me with emotions that I recognised, afterwards, as purely artistic. The sorriest pirate, the most wretchedly concealed treasure, poor Captain Mayne Reid at his boldest gave me then the sensations that I now search for in the "Odyssey" or in the thought of it; and I looked into some of these shabby old tales years afterwards, and wondered how on earth I had managed to penetrate into "faëry lands forlorn" through such miserable stucco portals. And you, you say, extracted somehow or other, from Harrison Ainsworth's "Lancashire Witches," that essence of the unknown that you now find in Poe, and I expect that everybody who loves literature could gather similar recollections.

Well, it would be easy enough to solve the problem by saying that the emotions of children are of no consequence and don't count, but then I don't think that proposition is true. I think, on the contrary, that children, especially young children before they have been defiled by the horrors of "education," possess the artistic emotion in remarkable purity, that they reproduce, in a measure, the primitive man before he was defiled, artistically, by the horrors of civilisation. The ecstasy of the artist is but a recollection, a remnant from the childish vision, and the child undoubtedly looks at the world through "magic casements." But you see all this is unconscious, or subconscious (to a less degree it is so in later life, and artists are rare simply because it is their almost impossible task to translate the emotion of the sub-consciousness into the speech of consciousness), and as you may sometimes see children uttering their conceptions in words that are nonsense, or next door to it, so nonsense or at any rate very poor stuff suffices with them to summon up the vision from the depths of the soul. Suppose we could catch a genius at the age of nine or ten and request him to utter what he felt; the boy would speak or write rubbish, and in the same way you would find that he read rubbish, and that it excited in him an ineffable joy and ecstasy. Coleridge was a Bluecoat boy when he read the "poems" of William Lisle Bowles, and admired them to enthusiasm, and I am quite sure that at some early period Poe had been enraptured by Mrs Radcliffe, and we know how Burns founded himself on Fergusson. When men are young, the inward ecstasy, the "red powder of projection" is of such efficacy and virtue that the grossest and vilest matter is transmuted for them into pure gold, glistering and glorious as the sun. The child (and with him you may link all primitive and childlike people) approaches books and pictures just as he approaches nature itself and life; and a wonderful vision appears where many of us can only see the common and insignificant.

But all this has been a digression; it has come by the way in a talk about worthless and insignificant books. But I think that we should by this time have brought our testing apparatus into working order; we should be able to criticise any given book on some ground or principle, not on the rule of thumb of "it sent me to sleep," or "it kept me awake." And I think that what I have already remarked about the subconscious element in literature should have answered that question about "books with a purpose." As a matter of fact I believe that they are mostly trash, but it is not a case for à priori reasoning; you must test each book by itself. Mr Stevenson was, I believe, an artist at heart, but we have seen how the artificer overcame the artist in "Jekyll and Hyde," and in like manner there have been cases of people who were artificers, and even preachers, at heart, who were forced to succumb to the concealed, subconscious artist, when pen touched paper. For example; first logically analyze "Lycidas"; you will be disgusted just as Dr Johnson, who had no analysis but the logical, was disgusted. Forget your logic, your common-sense, and read it again as poetry; you will acknowledge the presence of an amazing masterpiece. An unimportant lament over an unimportant personage, constructed on an affected pseudo-pastoral plan, full of acrid, Puritanical declamation and abuse, wantonly absurd with its mixture of the nymphs and St Peter; it is not only wretched in plan but clumsy in construction, the artifice is atrocious. And it is also perfect beauty! It is the very soul set to music; its austere and exquisite rapture thrills one so that I could almost say: he who understands the mystery and the beauty of "Lycidas" understands also the final and eternal secret of art and life and man.

IV

Doyou know that when we last talked belles lettres the whole evening went by (or at least I think so) without my saying anything about "Pickwick"? I hope you noted the omission in your diary, if you keep one, because I find it difficult to talk much about literature, without drawing some illustration from that very notable, and curious, and unappreciated book. Yes, I maintain the justice of the last epithet in spite of circulation, in spite of popularity, and in spite of "Pickwick 'literature.'" You may like a book very much and read it three times a year without appreciating it, and if a great book is really popular it is sure to owe its popularity to entirely wrong reasons. There are people, you know, who study Homer every day, because he throws so much light on the manners and customs of the ancients, and if a book of our own time is both great and popular, you may be sure that it is loved for its most peccant parts, just as nine people out of ten will recall the "Raven" and the "Bells" if the poetry of Edgar Allan Poe is mentioned.

After all, I needn't have excused myself for my constant references to Dickens's masterpiece, since I have already informed you that, like Coleridge, I love a "cyclical" mode of discoursing; and I honestly think that if you want to understand something about the Mysteries or the Fine Arts (which are the expression of the mysteries) it is the only way. A proposition in Euclid is demonstrated and done with, since nothing can be added to a mathematical proof; but literature is different. It is many-sided and many-coloured, and variable always; you can consider it in half-a-dozen ways, from half-a-dozen standpoints, and from half-a-dozen judgments, each of which will be true and perfect in itself, and yet each will supplement the other. Two or three weeks ago I think I tried to show you what a complex organism any given book reveals, if one examines it with a little attention, and if one specimen be so curiously and intricately fashioned, you may imagine the complexity of the whole subject.

But I have a more particular reason for turning once more to the "Posthumous Papers." We have noted that that which at first sight seems significant, may turn out to be insignificant, and I think that in passing I hinted that the reverse was sometimes the case. Very good; and the especial instance that is in my mind is the enormous capacity for strong drink exhibited by Mr Pickwick and all his friends and associates. Of course you've noticed it; perhaps you have thought it a nuisance and a blemish from the artistic standpoint, just as many "good people" have found it a nuisance and a blemish from the temperance or teetotal standpoint. You may have felt quite certain that a set of men who were always drinking brandy and water, and strong ale, and milk-punch, and madeira, who constantly drank a great deal too much of each and all of these things, would be extremely unpleasant companions in private life; I daresay you have been thankful that you never knew Mr Pickwick or any of his followers. You know, I expect, by personal experience, that a man whose daily life is a pilgrimage from one whiskey bar to another is, in most cases, an extremely tedious and unprofitable companion; and it is undeniable that the "Pickwickians" rather made opportunities for brandy and water than avoided them. And in an indirect manner, you feel that all this makes you like the book less.

But (I can no more miss an opportunity of digression than Mr Pickwick could keep on the coach if there were a chance of drinking his favourite beverage) do you know that there are really people who make their liking or disliking of the characters the criterion of literature—of romances, I mean? We touched on this some time ago, and I remember saying that in the case of such secondary books as Jane Austen's and Thackeray's, it was permissible enough to go where one was best amused, that one had a right to say, "Yes, the artifice may be the better here, but the characters are much more amusing there, and I had rather talk to the cosmopolitan whose manners are now and then a little to seek, than to the maiden lady in the village, whose decorum is so unexceptionable." But I confess that at the time it had not dawned upon me that there are people who try to judge fine art—the true literature—on the same grounds. I believe, however, that such is the case; I believe, indeed, that the egregious M. Voltaire was dimly moved by some such feeling when he wrote his famous "criticism" of the prophet Habakkuk. What (he must have said to himself) would they think in the salons of a man who talked like this:—

> And the everlasting mountains were scattered,
> The perpetual hills did bow:
> His ways are everlasting?

Evidently Habakkuk could never hope for a second invitation; and therefore he wrote rubbish. And I believe, as I said, that there are many people who more or less unconsciously judge literature by this measure, by asking, "Would these people be pleasant to meet? would one like to hear this kind of thing in one's drawing-room?" And this is well enough with secondary books, since they contain nothing but "characters," and "incidents," and "scenes," and "facts"; but it is by no means well in literature, in which, as we found out, all these things are symbols, words of a language, used, not for themselves, but because they are significant. Remember our old definition—ecstasy, the withdrawal, the standing apart from common life—and you will see that we may almost reverse this popular method of judgment, and turn it into another test, or rather another way of putting the test, of art. For, if literature be a kind of withdrawal from the common atmosphere of life, we shall naturally expect to find its utterance, both in matter and manner, wholly unsuitable for the drawing-room or the street, and its "characters" persons whom we cannot imagine ourselves associating with on pleasant or comfortable terms. Neither you nor I would be very happy on Ulysses's boat, we should soon become irritated with Don Quixote, we should hardly feel at home with Sir Galahad. It is true that all the good there is in men is this—that at rare intervals, in certain lonely moments of exaltation they do feel for the time a faint stirring of the beautiful within them, and then they would adventure on the Quest of the Graal; but as you know few of us are saints, fewer, perhaps, are men of genius; we are sunk for the most part of our days in the common life, and our care is for the body and for the things of the body, for the street and the drawing-room, and not for the perpetual, solitary hills. So you see that if you read a book and can say of the characters in it: "I wish I knew them," there is very strong reason to suspect that the book in question is not literature, though it may well be a pleasant picture of pleasant people.

Yes, I was expecting that question. I should have been sorry if your sense of humour had not prompted you to ask whether the drinking of too much milk-punch constituted a withdrawal from the common life, a profound and lonely ecstasy. But don't you remember that when we were discussing "Pickwick" before, and comparing it with the "Odyssey," I suddenly deserted Homer, and brought in Sophocles? I think I contrasted, very briefly, the education of the dramatist with the education of the romance writer, the London of the 'twenties and 'thirties with the city of the Violet Crown, the fate of him,

$$\text{ἀεὶ διὰ λαμπροτάτου}$$
$$\text{βαίνοντος ἁβρῶς αἰθέρος}$$

with that of the other who tried to find the way through the evil and hideous London fog.

Well, you might have been inclined to ask, why Sophocles? But do you remember for whose festivals, in whose honour the Greek wrote his dramas and his choral songs? It was the god of wine who was worshipped and invoked at the Dionysiaca, in the praise of Dionysus the chorus sang and danced about the altar, and all the drama arose from the celebration of the Bacchic mysteries. So you get, I think, a pretty fair proportion: as the Athens of Sophocles is to the Cockneydom of Dickens, so is the cult of Dionysus to the cult of cold punch and brandy and water. The interior meaning is in each case the same; the artistic expression has lamentably deteriorated, in the degree that the artistic atmosphere on the banks of Fleet Ditch, the "mother of dead dogs," was inferior to the artistic atmosphere on the banks of the Ilissus.

I expect you have gathered from all this talk the point I want to make: that the brandy and water and punch business in "Pickwick," which at first sight seems trivial and insignificant and even disgusting, is, in fact, full of the highest significance. Don't you notice the insistence with which the writer dwells on drinking, the unction and enthusiasm with which he describes it? We have admitted the poverty of the "materials" with which Dickens works, and of course it would be as idle to expect him to write a choral song in honour of Dionysus as it would be to expect him to write in

67

Greek. He expressed himself as best he could, in the "language" (that is with the incidents and in the atmosphere) that he knew, but there can be no possible doubt as to his meaning. In a word, I absolutely identify the "brandy and water scenes" with the Bacchic cultus and all that it implies.

This is "a little too much for you" is it? Well, let us take another well-known book, the "Gargantua" and "Pantagruel." You know it well, and I have only to remind you of the name to remind you that as "Pickwick" has been said to "reek with brandy and water," so does Rabelais assuredly reek of wine. The history begins:—

> "Grandgousier estoit bon raillard en son temps, aimant à boire net,"

it ends with the Oracle of the Holy Bottle, with the word

> "Trinch ... un mot panomphée, celebré et entendu de toutes nations, et nous signifie, beuvez;"

and I refer you to the allocution of Bacbuc, the priestess of the Bottle, at large. "By wine," she says, "is man made divine," and I may say that if you have not got the key to these Rabelaisian riddles much of the value —the highest value—of the book is lost to you. You know how they drink, those strange figures, the giants and their followers, you know the aroma of the vintage, the odour of the wine vat that fills all those marvellous and enigmatic pages, and I tell you that here again I recognise the same signs as in "Pickwick," the same music as that of the dithyrambic choruses in honour of Dionysus, which were eventually amplified into that magnificent literary product, the Greek drama. And if we wish to penetrate the secret we must not forget the Hebrew psalmist, with his calix meus inebrians quam præclarus est. And remember, too, if you feel inclined to shudder at the milk-punch, that the words which I have just quoted might be rendered, "how splendid is this cup of wine that makes me drunk!" and we may say that, in a manner, poor Dickens did so render them, since, as I have reminded you he belonged, after the flesh, to the Camden Town of the 'twenties, and was forced to use its unbeautiful dialect because he knew no other.

And after all, then, what does this Bacchic cultus mean? We have seen that under various disguises the one spirit appeared in Greece, in the France of the Renaissance, and in Victorian England, and that in each instance there is an apparent glorification of drunkenness. The Greeks, indeed, a sober people by necessity, as all Southerners are, impersonated the genius of intoxication, and made excessive drinking, as it would seem, an elaborate religion, with rites and festivals and mysteries. The Tourainian, whose personal habit was that not of a drunkard, but of a learned physician and restorer of ancient letters, who probably drank very much in the manner of the good curé I once knew ("My God!" he said to me, after the third small glass of small white wine, "'tis a veritable debauch!"), has, on the face of it, dedicated all his enormous book to the same cause, so that to read Pantagruel is like walking through a French village in the vintage season, when the whole world, as Zola unpleasantly and nastily expresses it "pue le raisin." Thirdly, Dickens, who loved to talk of concocting gin-punch, and left it, when concocted, to be drunk by his guests, shows us Mr Pickwick "dead drunk" in the wheel-barrow. And, for a final touch of apparent absurdity, you remember that the Dionysus myth represents wine as a civilising influence! You may well think of the public-house at the corner, and ask yourself how strong drink can contribute to civilisation.

Well, that is, in very brief outline, the problem and the puzzle; and I may say at once that to the literalist, the rationalist, the materialist

69

critic, the problem is quite insoluble. But to you and me, who do not end in any kind of ist, the enigma will not be quite so hopeless. Let us get back to our maxim that, in literature, facts and incidents are not present for their own sake but as symbols, as words of the language of art; it will follow, then, that the incidents of the Dionysus myth, the incidents of "Pantagruel" and "Pickwick" are not to be taken literally, but symbolically. We are not to conclude that the Greeks were a race of drunkards, or that Rabelais and Dickens preached habitual excess in drink as the highest virtue; we are to conclude that both the ancient people and the modern writers recognised Ecstasy as the supreme gift and state of man, and that they chose the Vine and the juice of the Vine as the most beautiful and significant symbol of that Power which withdraws a man from the common life and the common consciousness, and taking him from the dust of the earth, sets him in high places, in the eternal world of ideas. And, after all, I cannot do better than quote at length the sermon of Bacbuc, priestess of the Dive Bouteille.

> "Et icy maintenons que non rire, ains boire, est le propre de l'homme: je ne dis boire simplement et absolument, car aussi bien boivent les bestes: je dis boire vin bon et frais. Notez, amis, que de vin, divin on devient: et n'y a argument tant seur, ni art de divination moins fallace. Vos academiques l'afferment, rendans l'etymologie de vin lequel ils disent en Grec OINOΣ, estre comme vis, force, puissance. Car pouvoir il a d'emplir l'ame de toute verité, tout savoir et philosophie. Si avez noté ce qui est en lettres Ioniques escrit dessus la porte du temple, vous avez peu entendre qu'en vin est verité cachée."

You see how that passage lights up the whole book, and you see what Rabelais meant in the Prologue to the first book by that reference to "certain little boxes such as we see nowadays in apothecaries' shops, the which boxes are painted on the outside with joyous and fantastic figures ... but within they hold rare drugs, as balm, ambergris, amomum, musk, civet, certain stones of high virtue, and all manner of precious things." I do not know whether you have read any of our English commentators on Rabelais, if not, I would not advise you to do so, unless you take pleasure in futility. For instance they take the passage from the prologue, and seeing the hint that something is concealed, try by some complicated chain of argument to show that Rabelais veiled his attacks on the Church under a mask of "wild buffoonery." Of course the attacks on the Church (the "secondary" and comparatively unimportant element in the book, fairly answering to the attacks on books of Chivalry in the Don Quixote) are as open as any attack can well be, and anyone who finds a veil drawn between Rabelais' dislike for the clergy and his expression of it must have a very singular notion of what constitutes concealment, and a still more singular misapprehension of the motive-forces which make and shape great books. Art, you may feel quite assured, proceeds always from love and rapture, never from hatred and disdain, and satire of every kind qua satire is eternally condemned to that Gehenna where the pamphlets, the "literature of the subject," and the "life-like" books lie all together. In "Don Quixote" one perceives that Cervantes loved the romances he condemns, and the satire is therefore good-humoured, and, one may say, does his book little harm or none at all; but Rabelais had been harshly treated by the friars, and his consequent ill-humour, his very violent abuse are in disaccord with the eternal melodies which may be discerned in "Pantagruel," noted there under strange symbols. Yes, the satire in Rabelais is an "accident," which one has to accept and to make the best of; some of it is amusing enough, "joyous and fantastic," like the "apes and owls and antiques" that adorn the little boxes of the apothecaries, some of it is a little acrid, as I said; but let us never forget that the essence of the book is its splendid celebration of ecstasy, under the figure of the vine.

You know I have not opened the door; I have only put the key into your hands, in this as in other instances. There are things, which, strange to say, are better left unsaid, and this, no doubt, Rabelais perceived when he devised his symbolism and set many traps in the paths of the shallow commentator. It was not from dread of the consequences of attacking the clergy that he devised curious veils and concealments, since, as I have noted, his hatred of the church is quite open and unconcealed. He chose the method of symbolism, firstly because he was an artist, and symbolism is the speech of art; and secondly because the high truth that he prophesied was not, and is not, fit for vulgar ears. The secret places of the human nature are not heedlessly to be exposed to the uninitiated, who would merely profane this occult knowledge if they had it. By consequence the "Complete Works of Rabelais" are obtainable in Holywell Street, and many, seeking the libidinous, have found merely the tiresome, and have cursed their bargain.

No, I will positively say no more. The key is in your hands, and with it you may open what chambers you can. There is only this to be mentioned: that, if I were you, I would not be "afraid with any amazement" should Mr Pickwick's overdose of milk punch prove, ultimately, a clue to the labyrinth of mystic theology.

There are, however, one or two minor points in Rabelais that may be worth notice. I might, you know, analyze it as I attempted to analyze "Don Quixote." There is in "Gargantua" and "Pantagruel" that same complexity of thought and construction: you may note, first of all, the great essence which is common to these masterpieces as to all literature—ecstasy, expressed in the one case under the similitude of knight-errantry, in the other by the symbol of the vine. Then, in Rabelais you have another symbolism of ecstasy—the shape of gauloiserie, of gross, exuberant gaiety, expressing itself by outrageous tales, outrageous words, by a very cataract of obscenity, if you please, if only you will notice how the obscenity of Rabelais transcends the obscenity of common life; how grossness is poured out in a sort of mad torrent, in a frenzy, a very passion of the unspeakable. Then, thirdly, there is the impression one collects from the book: a transfigured picture of that wonderful age: there is the note of the vast, interminable argument of the schools, and for a respond, the clear, enchanted voice of Plato; there is the vision, there is the mystery of the vast, far-lifted Gothic quire; and those fair, ornate, and smiling châteaux rise smiling from the rich banks of the Loire and the Vienne. The old tales told in farmhouse kitchens in the Chinonnais, the exultation of the new learning, of lost beauty recovered, the joy of the vintage, the old legends, the ancient turns of speech, the new style and manner of speaking: so to the old world answers the new. Then one has the satire of clergy and lawyers—the criticism of life—analogous, as I said with much that is in Cervantes, and so from divers elements you see how a literary masterpiece is made into a whole.

But now, do you know, I am going to make a confession. You have heard me say more than once that in art, in literature properly so called, liking and disliking count for nothing. We have understood, I think, that when once amusing reading matter has been put out of court, the question of how often, with what absorption one reads a work of art, matters nothing. Well, I want to contradict, or rather to modify that axiom; we have been speaking of three great books, each of which I believe firmly to be true literature—"Pickwick,"

"Don Quixote," and "Pantagruel." Here is my confession. I read "Pickwick," say, once a year, "Don Quixote," once every three years, while I read Rabelais in fragments perhaps once in six years. You might suppose that I have indicated the order of merit? Well, I have, but you must reverse the order, since I firmly believe that "Pantagruel" is the finest of the three. We will leave Dickens out of account, since we are agreed that though the message was that of angels, the accent and the speech were of Camden town; he, that is to say, approaches most nearly to the common life, to the common passages in which we live, and hence he, naturally, pleases us the most in our ordinary and common humours. But, of the other two, I confess that Cervantes pleases me much the more; the vulgarity of Dickens is absent or rather it is concentrated in Sancho, in a much milder form than that of "Pickwick," for a Spanish peasant of the sixteenth century, with all his "common-sense," and practical reason, is less remote from beauty than the retired "business man" of the early nineteenth century; just as poor Mr Pickwick, an honest, kindly creature, is vastly superior to the blatant, pretentious, diamond-bedecked swindlers who represent the city in our day. But Cervantes, who lacks, as I say, the "commonness" of Dickens, has something of the urbanity, the cosmopolitanism of Thackeray, he is, to a certain degree, a Colonel Newcome of his time, but he has seen the world more sagaciously than Colonel Newcome ever could. So while Rabelais appals me with his extravagance, his torrents of obscene words, I am charmed with the good humoured and observant companionship of Cervantes.

And hence I conclude that "Pantagruel" is the finer book. It may sound paradoxical to say so, but don't you see that the very grotesquerie of Rabelais shows a further remove from the daily round, a purer metal, less tinged with the personal, material, interest than "Don Quixote." Mind you, I find greater deftness, a finer artifice in Cervantes, who I think expressed his conception the more perfectly, but I think that the conception of Rabelais the higher, precisely because it is the more remote. Look at the "Pantagruel"; consider those "lists," that more than frankness, that ebullition of grossness, plainly intentional, designed: it is either the merest lunacy, or else it is sublime. Don't you remember the trite saying "extremes meet," don't you perceive that when a certain depth has been passed you begin to ascend into the heights? The Persian poet expresses the most transcendental secrets of the Divine Love by the grossest phrases of the carnal love; so Rabelais soars above the common life, above the streets and the gutter by going far lower than the streets and the gutter: he brings before you the highest by positing that which is lower than the lowest, and if you have the prepared, initiated mind, a Rabelaisian "list" is the best preface to the angelic song. All this may strike you as extreme paradox, but it has the disadvantage of being true, and perhaps you may assure yourself of its truth by recollecting the converse proposition — that it is when one is absorbed in the highest emotions that the most degrading images will intrude themselves. No; you are right: this is not the psychology of the "scientific" persons who write hand-books on the subject, it is not the psychology of the "serious" novelists, of those who write the annals of the "engaged"; but it happens to be the psychology of man.

I don't know that very much can be made of the signification of the characters in "Pantagruel," as I hardly think that Rabelais was anxious to be systematic or consistent in delineating them. I believe that there are two reasons for the gigantic stature of Pantagruel, or perhaps three. The form of the whole story came from popular legends about a giant named Gargantua, and that is the first and least important reason. Secondly the "giant" conception does something to remove the book from common experience; it is a sign-post, warning you not to expect a faithful picture of life, but rather a withdrawal from life and from common experience, and you are in a position to appreciate the value of that motive, since I have never ceased from telling you that it is the principal motive of all literature. And, thirdly, I hesitate and doubt, but nothing more, whether the giant Pantagruel, he who is "all thirst" and ever athirst, may not be a hint of the stature of the perfect man, of the ideal man, freed from the bonds of the common life, and common appetites, having only the eternal thirst for the eternal vine. Candidly, I am inclined to favour this view, but only as a private interpretation; it may be all nonsense, and I shall not be offended or surprised if you can prove to me that it is nonsense. But have you noticed how Pantagruel is at once the most important and the least important figure in the book? He is the most important personage; he is the hero, the leader, the son of the king, the giant, wiser than any or all of his followers: formally, he is to Rabelais that which Don Quixote is to Cervantes. And yet, actually, he is little more than a vague, tremendous shadow; the living, speaking, impressive personages are Frère Jean and Panurge, who occupy the stage and capture our attention. Doesn't this rather suggest to you the part played by the "real" man in life itself; a subordinate, unobtrusive part usually, hidden very often by an exterior, which bears little resemblance to the true man within. You know Coleridge says that:—

"Pantagruel is the Reason; Panurge the Understanding—the pollarded man, the man with every faculty except the reason. I scarcely know an example more illustrative of the distinction between the two. Rabelais had no mode of speaking the truth in those days but in such form as this; as it was, he was indebted to the king's protection for his life."

I must cavil at the last sentence, in which Coleridge seems to hint that Rabelais was in danger because he had hinted the distinction between the Reason and the Understanding. With all respect to Coleridge, Rabelais might have gone to the limits of psychology and metaphysics without incurring any danger; he was threatened on account of his very open satire of the church and the clergy, which, as I have pointed out, is as plain spoken as satire well can be. Still, I think that Coleridge, using the technical language of German philosophy, had a glimpse of the truth, and Mr Besant's remark that Panurge is a careful portrait of a man without a soul is virtually the same definition in another terminology. As I have already said, I don't think that Rabelais kept his characters within the strict limits of consistence — they are only significant, perhaps, now and then — and I want to say, again, that I speak under correction in this matter, not feeling at all sure of my ground. But I am inclined to think that Pantagruel, Panurge, and the Monk are not so much three different characters, as the representative of man in his three persons. Frère Jean is, perhaps, the natural man, the "healthy animal," Panurge is the rational man, and Pantagruel, as I said, is the spiritual, or perfect man, who looms, gigantic, in the background, almost invisible, and yet all important, and the three are, in reality, One. If I may apply the case to our own subject, I may say that while Pantagruel conceives the idea, Panurge writes the book, and Brother John has the courage to take it to the publishers. The first is the artist, the second the artificer, and the third the social being, ready to battle for his place in the material world. The giant is always calm, since his head is high above earth — vidit nubes et sidera — but the other two have to face the compromises of life, and suffer its defeats. All this may be purely fantastical; and at any rate I am sure that anyone who knows his Rabelais could pick many holes in my interpretation. For example, I said that the monk was the "healthy animal," and Panurge the rational man; but there are occasions when Panurge assumes the character of the unhealthy beast, the hairy-legged, hybrid, creature of the Greek myth, who uses the superior human artifice for ends that are wholly bestial or worse than bestial. Still; is this a valid objection? Are there not such men in life itself? Is it not, perhaps, the peculiar and terrible privilege of humanity that it may, if it pleases, prostitute its most holy and most blessed gifts to the worst and most horrible uses? And does not each one of us feel that, potentially, at all events, there is such a being within him, not yielded to, perhaps, for a moment, yet always present, always ready to assume the command. The greatest saints, we are told, have suffered the most fiery temptations; in other words— Pantagruel is always attended by Panurge diabolicus. I have talked once or twice of the Shadowy Companion, but one must not forget that there is the Muddy Companion also; a being often of exquisite wit and deep understanding, but given to evil ways if one do not hold him in check.

But, in any case, I think I have shown that the Pantagruel is one of the most extraordinary efforts of the human mind, full of "Pantagruelism"; and that word stands for many concealed and wonderful mysteries.

It is not in the least a "pleasant," or a "life-like," or even an "interesting" book; I think that when one knows of the key—or rather of the keys—one opens the pages almost with a sensation of dread. So it is a book that one consults at long intervals, because it is only at rare moments that a man can bear the spectacle of his own naked soul, and a vision that is splendid, certainly, but awful also, in its constant apposition of the eternal heights and the eternal depths.

V

I have been waiting for that question for a very long time, and I only wonder that you have been able to restrain yourself so well — through such a series of what I know you believe to be paradoxes, though I have assured you that I deal merely in the plainest truth. But, after all, your question is quite a legitimate one, and I remember when I first began to think of these things I went astray — simply because I did not recognise the existence of the difficulty that has been bothering you, ever since that talk of ours about the haulte sagesse Pantagrueline — et Pickwickienne, and perhaps before it.

Yes, I will put the question in its plainest, crudest form, and I will make you ask, if you please, whether Charles Dickens had any consciousness of the interior significance of the milk-punch, strong ale, and brandy and water which he caused Mr Pickwick and his friends to consume in such outrageous quantities. It sounds plain enough and simple enough, doesn't it, and yet I must tell you that to answer that question fairly you must first analyze human nature, and I needn't remind you that that is a task very far from simple. "Man" sounds a very simple predicate, as you utter it; you imagine that you understand its significance perfectly well, but when you begin to refine a little, and to bring in distinctions, and to carry propositions to their legitimate bounds, you find that you have undertaken the definition of that which is essentially indefinite and probably indefinable. And, after all, we need not pitch on this term or on that, there is no need to select "man" as offering any especial difficulty, for, I take it, that the truth is that all human knowledge is subject to the same disadvantage, the same doubts and reservations. Omnia exeunt in mysterium was an old scholastic maxim; and the only people who have always a plain answer for a plain question are the pseudo-scientists, the people who think that one can solve the enigma of the universe with a box of chemicals.

But all this is a caution—necessary I suppose—that you need not expect me to give you a plain, cut and dried answer to your question whether literature is a conscious production—or, in more particular form—was Dickens aware that by milk-punch he meant ecstasy? I shall "ask you another" in the approved Scotch manner. You were telling me that as you came along this evening you had to stop for five minutes at the corner of the Caledonian Road to watch the exquisite grace of two slum-girls of fourteen or fifteen, dancing to the rattling tune of a piano-organ. You spoke of the charm of their movements—motus Ionici, some of them, I fear—of the purely æsthetic delight there was in the sight of young girls, disguised as horrible little slatterns, leaping and dancing as young girls have always leapt and danced, I suppose, from the time of the cave-dwellers onwards. Well, but do you suppose that this charm you have remarked was conscious? Do you think that Harriet and Emily realised that they were of the kin of the ecstatic dancers of all time, that they were beautiful because they were naturally expressing by a symbol that is universal, the universal and eternal ecstasy of life? Look back in your memory for illustrations; I, as you know, am rather the enemy of facts, and it is rarely that I am able to support a theory by a systematic catena of instances and authorities. But, if one had the industry and energy, one might make a most curious history of the dance. Remember the Hebrew dances of religious joy, of ecstasy in its highest form, remember that strange survival of the choristers' dance before the high altar in Spain on certain solemn feasts, a survival which has persisted in spite of the strong Roman influences which make for rigid uniformity. Think of the Greek Menads and Bacchantes, of the Dionysiac chorus in the theatre, of our old English peasants "treading the mazes," and dancing round the maypole, of dances at Breton Pardons, of the fairies, supposed to dance in the forest glade beneath the moon. Why, dancing is as much an expression of the human secret as literature itself, and I expect it is even more ancient; and Harriet and Emily, leaping on the pavement, to that jingling, clattering tune, were merely showing that though they were the children of the slum, and the step-children of the School Board, they were yet human, and partakers of the universal sacrament.

But if you ask, were they conscious of all this, it will be very difficult to give a direct answer. I need hardly say that they could not have put their very real emotion into the terms I have used — nor perhaps into any terms at all — and yet they know the delight of what they do, as much as if they had been initiated in all the mysteries. If someone with the genius of Socrates for propounding searching questions could "corner" Harriet and Emily, and face and overcome that preliminary, inevitable "garn," it is possible that he might find that they were fully conscious of the reasons why they danced and delighted in dancing; just as Socrates demonstrated to the slave that he was perfectly acquainted with geometry; but failing a Socrates, and using words in their usual senses, I suppose we must say that they are not conscious. They dance and leap without calculation, as they eat and drink, and as birds sing in springtime; and very much the same answer must be given to the similar question as to literature.

I said that to answer the riddle fully and completely, one would have to make an analysis of human nature; and, in truth, the problem is simply a problem of the consciousness and

81

subconsciousness, and of the action and interaction between the two. I will not be too dogmatic. We are in misty, uncertain and unexplored regions, and it is impossible to chart all the cities and mountains and streams, and fix with the nicety of the ordnance survey their several places on the map—but I am strangely inclined to think that all the quintessence of art is distilled from the subconscious and not from the conscious self; or, in other words, that the artificer seldom or never understands the ends and designs and spirit of the artist. Our literary architects have all, I think, builded better than they knew, and very often, I expect, the draughtsman who sees the triumph and enjoys it in his manner, takes all the credit to himself, and ludicrously imagines that it is his careful drawing and amplification of the sketch, and following the scale, that have created the high and holy house of God. There is a queer instance of what I mean in Dickens's preface to the later editions of "Pickwick"—I put the book up on a high shelf the other day, and I can't be bothered getting it down and verifying the quotation—but I believe the author, after telling us that the original design was to give opportunities to the etcher Seymour, goes on to recapitulate, as it were, the achievements of the book, and his list of triumphs is much more amusing than any list in Rabelais. The law of imprisonment for debt has been altered! Fleet Prison has been pulled down! The School-Board is coming! Lawyers' clerks have nicer manners! Parliamentary elections are a little better, but they might be better still! and one wonders that he does not announce that, in consequence of the publication of "Pickwick," medical students have given up brandy for barley-water. It is evident, you see, that Dickens thought (or thought that he thought, for it is very difficult to be exact) that his masterpiece of the picaresque, his epitome of Pantagruelism, was written to correct abuses, and looking back, many years after its publication, he congratulates himself that most of these abuses have been corrected, and (one can almost hear him say) ergo, it is a very fine book. He was impelled to write this nonsense of the preface because he was, by comparison, "educated"; Harriet, the dancer, would probably tell you, if you succeeded in penetrating beyond "garn," that she danced because she liked it; but, granting that the poisoning process had been carried out more successfully in the case of Emily, she might, conceivably, reply that she danced "becos it's 'elthy, and Teacher says as 'ow it cirkilates the blood." Emily, you see, obtained the prize for Physiology, as well as for French and the Piano-Forte; she is thus enabled to give "reasons," and they are quite as valuable as the "reasons" of Dickens, explaining the merits of "Pickwick." You know that pompous old fool Forster, who took in Dickens at times, sniffed a little at "Pickwick," and thought the later books, with their ingenious plots, and floods of maudlin tears, and portentous "character-drawing," immense advances, and I suppose the master felt obliged to justify himself for that first enterprise—to show that he had not really been inspired, but had written a useful tract! You remember he "explains" Stiggins; he warns you not to be under any misconceptions, not to suppose that Stiggins satirises a, b, or c, since he is only aimed at x, y, and z. Can you conceive that a mediæval artist in gurgoyles, having perfected for our eternal joy, a splendid grinning creature, lurking on the parapet, and having endowed him, greatly to our oblectation, with the tail of a dragon, the body of a dog, the feet of an eagle, the head of a bull in hysterics, with a Franciscan cowl, by way of finish, should afterwards explain that no offence was intended to Father Ambrose, the prior over the way?

So it seems fairly plain, doesn't it, that in the case of Dickens, at all events, there was no very clear consciousness of what had been achieved, and I believe that you would find the rule hold good with other artists in a greater or less degree. With Dickens it holds in a very high degree, just because there was that tremendous gulf I have so often spoken about between his inward and his outward self; because, with the soul of rare genius, his intelligence lived in those dreary, dusty London streets, because the artificer, even while he carried out the artist's commands, understood very little what he was doing. But one can trace the same working in other cases. Take the case of Mr Hardy, for instance. You remember what I said about his "Two on a Tower"; I praised it for its ecstatic passion, for that revelation of a great rapture, for its symbolism, showing how one must withdraw from the common ways, from the dusty highroad and the swarming street, and go apart into high, lonely places, if one would perceive the high, eternal mysteries. I did not say so in so many words, but you no doubt saw that I was indicating that which is, in my opinion, valuable in Mr Hardy's work, that which makes his books literature. And I am sure he would most decidedly and entirely disagree with me, and if you want to know why I am sure, I refer you to his later books, to his "Tess" and "Jude." You know how the "Tess" was talked about, how it remade the author from the commercial standpoint, simply because it contained, with many beautiful things, many absurd "preachments," much pseudo-philosophy of a kind suited to the intelligence of persons who think that "Robert Elsmere" is literature. If Mr Hardy had been a conscious artist, if he had understood, I mean, what makes the charm and the wonder of "Two on a Tower," he could never have adulterated the tale of "Tess" with a free-thinking tract, he would never have turned "Jude" into a long pamphlet on secondary education for farm labourers, with agnostic notes. It is pathetic in the latter book amidst much weary and futile writing to come across a passage here and there that shows the artist striving for utterance, longing to sing us his incantations, in spite of the preacher, who howls him down. Think of that distant vision of Oxford from the lonely field, of all those clustering roofs and spires, wet with rain, suddenly kindling into glancing, and scintillant fire, at the sunset; and then remember, with what sorrow, that this is but an oasis in a barren land of blundering argument. It is almost as if literature had become "literature"—the "literature of the subject"—and one must only rejoice that the artist still lives even if the enemy has shut him up in prison. You can trace the struggle all through the book: "Sue" was an artistic conception, a very curious but a very beautiful revelation of some strange elements in the nature and in the love of women; but how difficult it is to detect this—the real Sue—underneath the surface, which makes Sue seem the prophetess of the "Woman Question," or whatever the contemporary twaddle on the subject was called. Conceive the "Odyssey" so handled that it seems like a volume in a "technical series" dealing with "Seamanship and Navigation," think what might have happened if the Rabelais who had been put in the dark cell of Fontenay-le-Comte had completely gained the upper hand, and had silenced that other Rabelais—that solitary and rapturous soul who had seen as in a glass the marvellous face of man. Well, the five books of the "Pantagruel" would have conveyed to us, no doubt with some eloquence and vigour, the highly unimportant fact that François Rabelais, runaway Franciscan friar, did not like Franciscan friars; and now that the centuries have gone by we see how (comparatively) worthless such a book as that would have been. Fortunately Pantagruel was too strong for the forces of Panurge and Frère Jean combined, and so they have been able to do little harm to the book.

85

And how one wishes that it might be so with Mr Hardy! It is not as if he had no "body" for his conceptions; his studies of peasant folk do very well as backgrounds for his dramas, though, of course, his work in this way, good as it is, is not his element of real value. But it is inoffensive always, sometimes amusing, and it might well suffice him in his more material moments, when he feels the necessity of descending from the solitary heights into the pleasant, populous valleys and villages of common life. But his true work is — as it is the work of all artists — the shaping for us of ecstasy by means of symbols; and for him the symbol which he understands is, no doubt, the passion of love, and with it the symbol of red, lonely ploughlands, of deep overshadowed lanes that climb the hills and wander into lands that we know not, of dark woods that hide a secret, of strange, immemorial barrows where one may have communion with the souls of the dead. The passion of love, the passion of the hills — no artist could desire more exquisite or significant symbols than these, nor need he seek for more beautiful forms for the expression of the perfect beauty. And Mr Hardy has chosen to be a pamphleteer, to voice for us our poor, ignorant contemporary chatter: it is as if an angel's pen were to be occupied in inditing "Society Small Talk!"

But it proves the unconsciousness of Mr Hardy's art; and here, by the way, I am moved to revert to the case of Rabelais. How far, you may ask, was he conscious of what he was saying, and I see you remember that passage I quoted from the last book — the splendid declaration of the Priestess Bacbuc that "by wine is man made divine." That passage, and indeed many other passages in the final chapters, would seem to show that the author had worked consciously, and I certainly think the point worth our consideration. You will remember that I stated my rule without bigotry; I rather proposed it as a pious opinion—to the effect that in literature the finest things are not designed. And I confess, that at first sight, this matter of Bacbuc and her allocution looks rather like an exception to the rule, a proof that Rabelais, at all events, understood clearly what he was doing.

Well; it may have been so; for Rabelais was, as I think I have shown, a very exceptional man, whom it would be difficult to place in any class. But I hardly think this is an instance of the proverbial (and fallacious) exception that proves the rule. In the first place I believe that some French editors have grave doubts whether Rabelais wrote the fifth book at all; but I am not inclined to press this point. My point is that the allocution of Bacbuc and all those chapters which describe the Oracle of the Holy Bottle are the last in the book—the last words of the author; and I am in no way concerned to defend the position that an author must always remain unconscious of the work that he has done. As a matter of fact I think that always, or almost always, he is unconscious while he is writing; but I see no reason why the revelation may not come to him afterwards, especially in such a case as the "Pantagruel," which was the affair of many years—of a lifetime, indeed. In the beginning of production, in the youth, the springtime of artistic work, the creative influence prevails, and this, it seems to me, always or almost always operates secretly; but in later years the critical spirit is apt to assert itself, and this will lead, very naturally, to the artist's understanding more plainly the nature of his accomplishment. Rabelais had a long, wonderful career; his life was full of incident, of violent breaks, and his books were produced at intervals, and it seems to me very possible that, towards the end, he may have reflected on what he had done, and have understood in part, at all events, the sense of the amazing message that he had delivered. This, I think, is the explanation of the "Holy Bottle" chapters, and you will note that, admirable as criticism, they are inferior as art to those astounding early pages where there is no hint of conscious workmanship, but rather evidence of a man for whom the world has been transformed, who has been visited by an astounding vision. He takes an old, popular story about a giant, he takes the vine that flourishes in his native Chinonnais, he takes the New Learning that seems to him like the New Wine, he takes the gross tale of the farmhouse and the tavern, the rank speech of the people, and with these elements, with these "facts," he symbolises the revelation that he has received. He writes, he writes on, he writes madly, and every line is written in a fury of delight; but, I think I may say, there is at the moment of writing, no conscious apperception of all that that torrent of words conveys and implies. That may well come later; one may well begin with legend: "Grandgousier was a good drinker," and end with the interpretation: "All truth and every philosophy is contained in wine"; but I believe that if Rabelais had perceived this at the beginning he would have been not an artist but a philosopher.

Well; if you are content with this comment on Bacbuc, I should like to give you a very curious instance of our own day, in which the unconscious artist has been subdued by the conscious preacher. You remember those very notable books: "Keynotes" and "Discords"? I have not seen them for some time, so I am afraid my criticism will be very loose and general, but I think that the two volumes mark very well the fatal descent from the higher to the lower ground. In the first, it seems to me, there is a somewhat slight, but very genuine, note of ecstasy; I mean that you can collect a certain distinct image of real womanhood—not the laboured, foolish, inane psychology of Mr Meredith and those who work with him—not the analysis of the surface, of the "society" woman, belonging to a particular grade, and a particular period, but of the very woman who remains really the same in all social grades and in all ages. I remember thinking when I read "Keynotes" that it was a "lonely" book; it hinted, I think, a soul apart, and afar from the secondary, tertiary problems of an organised civilisation, and though there was an undertone of "preaching" and arguing, the total impression was curiously and beautifully artistic. I found, if I remember rightly, that subordination of the accidental to the essential that I praised in "Two in a Tower," and I am the more convinced that this is so by my own recollections. I have forgotten all about social conditions, if any such things are indicated; I only think of women and of men, of the true, inalterable human nature; and here, it seems to me, you have a very high achievement. But the next volume "Discords" took distinctly lower ground. The artifice was better, the stories, as stories, were told with more skill and more deftness than anything in "Keynotes"; but there was no more literature; there was only the "literature of the subject." The incidents were no longer symbols of an emotion; they had become the basis of an agitation, concerning which my curiosity never led me to inquire further: and there you see another proof of the unconsciousness of art. If the author of "Keynotes" had understood her achievement "Discords" would never have been written. One might continue the catena almost ad infinitum: would not Wordsworth, supposing him to have been a conscious artist, have rather cut off his right hand than have suffered such a magisterium as the "Ode on Intimations of Immortality" to have the companionship of the enormous mass of futility and stupidity which constitutes the greater part of the "Complete Works"?

Well, there is the evidence that must guide us in answering the question you propounded, and it shows, conclusively enough, I think, that art is not, in the ordinary acceptation of the term, a conscious product. Perhaps it would be a perilous dogmatism, on the other hand, to definitely pronounce it to be unconscious; and I expect we had better take refuge in the subconscious, that convenient name for the transcendental element in human nature. For myself, I like best my old figure of the Shadowy Companion, the invisible attendant who walks all the way beside us, though his feet are in the Other World; and I think that it is he who whispers to us his ineffable secrets, which we clumsily endeavour to set down in mortal language. I think that while the artist works he is conscious of joy and of nothing more; he works beautifully but he could give no rationale of the process, and when he endeavours to explain himself, we are often perplexed by this strange spectacle of a man wholly ignorant of his own creation. Consider again the grotesqueness of that preface to "Pickwick"; it is really as if a great sculptor, congratulated on his achievement, should answer that his Venus was indeed beautiful—because it tended to improve the marble industry and the general knowledge of anatomy.

And after all the conclusion does return to us from other than literary sources. You cannot conceive a builder of the fourteenth century hesitating as to the respective merits of Romanesque, Norman, First and Second Pointed; to him there was only one possible method, and he built, as he spoke, without calculation and without conscious effort, only knowing the joy of his work. So indeed we all speak and live when we are not bound by convention and acquired usages and manners, and you see that art, properly so called, takes its place in the great scheme of things; it is no studied contortion, no strange trick acquired by the late ingenuity of man, but as "natural" (and as supernatural) as the blossoming of a flower, and the singing of the nightingale. Art, indeed, is wholly natural, artifice is more or less acquired, the creature of reason, of experiment, of systematised intelligence. It is doubtful, I suppose, whether the natural, untaught man has of himself, by endowment, any artifice at all; doubtful, perhaps, whether, in the beginning, his artifice was not the product of his art; whether he did not learn to speak with artifice because he had received from nature the art of singing; certainly the child, entering the world, has not the inborn artifice of the swallow and the bee. This artifice, it seems, man has been forced to acquire by slow and painful degrees, and perhaps it only differs from the artifice of animals in that it has been aided and reinforced by imagination, that is by art, that is by the power the human soul possesses of projecting itself into the unknown, and adventuring in the realm of nothingness. Man, I mean, could never have invented the telephone, had he not first created it, had he not conceived the possibility of its existence, when as yet, it was non-existent, and so his artifice will always be progressive, and distinguished from the artifice of animals.

But art is born with man, and is of the essence, the very differentia of man. It is of his very inmost being, and therefore, I suppose, is removed from his consciousness simply because it is within and not from without. You may say that I have been vague, that I have not solved the problem I propounded, that I have not clearly explained whether the Greeks knew what they did when they worshipped Dionysus, whether Rabelais was conscious of an inner meaning in his praise of wine, whether Dickens understood the value of his punch and brandy. But if I have been vague it is because man, in the last analysis, is a tremendous mystery, because he is a complex being, because he is at once Pantagruel, and Panurge, and Frère Jean, because he is both Don Quixote and Sancho Panza. In some cases Pantagruel and Panurge seem to speak a common language, to be able to communicate the one with the other: if Rabelais wrote the "Dive Bouteille" chapters, he certainly understood much of that which he had expressed in symbols. Sometimes the two seem like foreigners in one home, Pantagruel dictates, and Panurge the scribe writes down his words, hardly or not at all comprehending the magic symbols that he expresses. So Dickens ludicrously misinterprets his own "Pickwick." And, doubtless, this understanding of the artificer of the artist varies in an almost infinite chain of nuances: there have been artists, perhaps, who have worked like men under the influence of haschish, who have opened their mouths and prophesied, and then recovering from the possession, have sat up and stared, and asked where they were, and what they had been doing. Indeed, it may be that this was the condition of the working of art in the very dawn of human life, for this, no doubt, is the explanation of that old equation in which bards, magicians, seers, prophets, and madmen ranked all together as men who spoke and worked miracles, things unintelligible to the "common sense," to the understanding which regulates and arranges the affairs of the common life. All these were alike men of the mountains, men who withdrew from the camp, and went apart into high solitary places, into the lonely wilderness, into the forest, and in such retirements and cells they uttered the voices that came to them, speaking words that were unintelligible to themselves.

On the other hand there may have been artists in whom the two persons have been happily reconciled, who have not only the "gift of tongues" but also the gift of the interpretation of tongues. Even these, I think, are always "possessed," ecstatic, rapt from their common nature at the moment of inspiration, but afterwards, when the magic song is done, they awake and return and remember, and understand, in a measure at least, the meaning of their prophecies. They never wholly understand, they are never able to express in rational terms the whole force of the message, for the good reason that the language of the soul infinitely transcends the language of the understanding; because art is, indeed, the sole channel by which the highest and purest truth can reach us. You may, perhaps, succeed in giving a Boer "some notion" of a Greek chorus through the medium of the "Taal," but it would be vain to dream of translating almost perfect beauty into that poor medium, framed for the temporary and corporal necessities of rough and illiterate farmers. And so, however well an artist or those who appreciate his work may "understand" his meaning, they do but "understand" a little; since the tongue of art has many words which have no rendering in the speech of the understanding.

Here, then, is another form of our text which enables us to separate art from artifice, literature from reading matter. Artifice is explicable; you remember that someone has said Thackeray was simply the ordinary clubman plus genius and a style. We must correct his phrases: but if you substitute an "immense talent of observation" for genius, and a "great gift of expression" for style, I think the definition admirable. Thackeray, in short, is the clubman of heightened faculties; he differs not in quiddity but in quality and quantity from his neighbour at the window; he looks more closely than Tom Eaves, and he can give you the result of his inspection in better phrases and with a better system, but he looks at the same things from the same standpoint, and you and I can admire his work and be amused and delighted by it, but we have no sense of miracle, of transcendent vision and achievement. We simply see a man who does the things that we do, but does them with a far greater dexterity: you may watch an acrobat with an immense admiration, but you recognise that you, too, are potentially an acrobat, that with a little training you, too, could hang by the heels, though not with such grace, nor for so long a time.

But art is always miraculous. In its origin, in its working, in its results it is beyond and above explanation, and the artist's unconsciousness is only one phase of its infinite mysteries.

VI

I am afraid that at our last conversation I rather spoke to you "as if you were a public meeting." Not precisely in that manner, perhaps, since no public meeting that I can imagine would have stood me for a moment, but I fear that I was what is called "high-flown." And yet how can one avoid that reproach? Look here: let us suppose an examination paper, and the following questions set.

1. Explain, in rational terms, the "Quest of the Holy Graal." State whether in your opinion such a vessel ever existed, and if you think it did not, justify your pleasure in reading the account of the search for it.

2. Explain, logically, your delight in colour. State, in terms that Voltaire would have understood, the meaning of the phrase, "the beauty of line."

3. What do you mean by the word "music"? Give the rational explanation of Bach's Fugues, showing them to be as (1) true as Biology and (2) useful as Applied Mechanics.

4. Estimate the value of Westminster Abbey in the Avoirdupois measure.

5. "The light that never was on land or sea." What light?

6. "Faery lands forlorn." Draw a map of the district in question, putting in principal towns, and naming exports.

7. Show that, "heaven lies about us in our infancy" must mean "wholesome maternal influences surround us in our childhood."

You say that is all nonsense? that one cannot express art of any kind in the terms of rationalism? Well, I agree with you that it is nonsense; that the tables of weights and measures give no æsthetic guide to the value of Westminster Abbey; but if we agree on this I am afraid that we must be content to be called high-flown. Having once for all settled that "common sense" has nothing to do with literary art, we must be, I suppose, uncommon, and (apparently) nonsensical if we want to talk about it to any profit. That is what it comes to, after all. If literature be a kind of dignified reporting, in which the reporter is at liberty to invent some incidents and leave out others, and to arrange all in the order that pleases him best; then, let us have as much "common sense" and "rationalism" as you please, and the more the better; but if literature is a mysterious ecstasy, the withdrawal from all common and ordinary conditions—well, I suppose, we had better be mystics when we discuss the subject, and frankly confess that with its first principles logic has nothing to do. I suppose that there are only two parties in the world: the Rationalists and the Mystics, and one's vote on literature goes with one's party. One might leave the matter there, and amiably agree to differ with the other side, but I, personally, have the ferocity to insist, that my side, the mystical, is wholly right, and the other, the rationalist, wholly wrong, and moreover I shall be so indecent as to prove the truth of my position. But, I have done so, and with that "Examination Paper" I just read out to you. For if rationalism be the truth, then all literature, all that both sides agree in thinking the finest literature is simple lunacy, and all the world of the arts must go into the region of mania. Take the lowest, the simplest instance. Here is a knife with a wooden handle, and the handle has certain curious carved designs on it, which do not enable it to be held better. Why is this knife better, more to be valued, than that other knife, which is not decorated at all? It does not cut better; it does not justify its existence and purpose as a knife more than the other; where is its superiority? Because I find pleasure in seeing those designs? But why do I find any pleasure in ornament? What is the rationalistic justification for that pleasure? By logical definition a knife is an instrument for cutting, and nothing else; the plain cuts as well as the ornate; why then are you sorry if you lose the one, while you don't care twopence for the loss of the other? You have at last to answer that you have a joy which you cannot in any way define in the purely decorative pattern; and with that answer the whole system of rationalism topples over. Rationalism may say to you: Either give a definite reason for going to Mass, or leave off going. You have only to answer: Your command is based on the premiss that one should do nothing without being able to give a definite reason for it. But I can give no definite reason for liking—the Odyssey or a curiously carved knife—and yet you confess that I am right in liking these things. Then I have proved the contradictory of your premiss, as you have admitted that there are things that one may do without being able to give a definite reason for doing them: ergo, I shall not neglect the "parson's bell."

Of course, all this is altogether outside of my business; but I confess I am fond of carrying things to their limits. You remember how poor S. T. C. used to talk, humbly and yet proudly, of "my system," though I am afraid "my system," never emerged from the state of fragments and disjecta membra. And I too, though I have only broken morsels and ruinous stones to show for the splendid outlines and indicated arches of Coleridge, still like to follow up an argument whithersoever it will lead me, regardless of consequences; and this, I am sure, should count for righteousness with our friends the rationalists. I love to start a sorites, something as follows: I admire that odd but beautiful little decorative scheme on the seventeenth century chest, and therefore, I think poetry, as poetry, finer than prose, as prose. Hence I approve of "Ritualism" in the service of the church, and from the same premiss I draw the conclusion that Keats was a poet and that Pope was not. Pope not being a poet, it follows that to "intone" is in every way better than to "read" the Liturgy and the Offices, and "reading" the service being wrong, you will easily infer that I dislike Mr Frith's pictures. And after learning that I do not care for the "Derby Day," you will scarcely require my opinion as to the (theoretical) righteousness of the first Reform Bill, and from my attitude towards Lord John Russell's measure, you can, of course, guess my opinion on the respective merits of the French and English languages as literary instruments. And French being vastly inferior to English, it necessarily follows that the English Reformation was a great (though perhaps unavoidable) misfortune. Hence, you see, admiring certain lines cut in an old oaken box, I am led by the strictest logic to dislike the religious policy of Edward VI., with all the other consequences in order; and on the other hand if I saw no sense in that rude ornament I should be an Atheist, or at the mildest, an attendant at Pleasant Sunday Afternoons, with George Eliot for my favourite reading.

Yes, I like my theories to "work through," and I confess that my belief in the truth of "my system" is very much strengthened by the fact that it does "work through," that it seems to me justified by the facts of life. I mean that the premiss which enables me to declare Keats to be a poet and Pope not to be a poet does really enable me to pronounce democracy to be a bad system in theory; and the premiss baldly stated is simply this: that logic does not cover life, or in other words, that life cannot be judged by the rules of logic, of common sense.

But yet I am using logic all the time, you say? Certainly, but I am using it in its right place, to do the work for which it is competent. If I say that a scythe is not exactly the instrument for performing a surgical operation, I am not therefore bound to have my meadow mown with a bistoury? A microscope is good and a telescope is good, but it is the microscope that one uses in bacteriology. You know, don't you, that ever since that unhappy Reformation of ours people have been talking nonsense about the Aristotelian logic, and fumbling, in the most grotesque manner, for some "new ' logic. Our great false prophet Bacon (a wretch infinitely more guilty than Hobbes) began it in England with his "Novum Organum"; and if you wish to really estimate "educated" folly, to touch the bottom of the incredible depths to which a man of information may sink, read Macaulay's comparison of the "old" philosophy and the "new" philosophy. The essayist says that the "old" philosophy was no good, because it never led up to the steam-engine and the telegraph post. Isn't it almost humiliating to think that we have to acknowledge ourselves of the same genus as that "brilliant" Macaulay? But if I told you that the Greek Alphabet was no good because it has never grilled a single steak you would probably get uneasy and make for the door, and if you were charitable you would tell the landlady that I ought to be "taken care of.' But such a remark as that is no whit more lunatic than Macaulay's "comparison" between philosophy, properly so called, and physical science applied to utilitarian purposes. Well, all the portentous stuff that has been written about logic is nonsense of exactly the same kind. The scholastic logic, people said, won't discover the truth. That is perfectly true, but then the scholastic logic was not intended to discover truth. It will draw conclusions from truths already discovered, from premises granted, but it wont make premisses any more than a scythe will make grass. And, it is, curiously enough, the very class of people who despise the formal logic, who insist on your giving logical reasons for actions and emotions which are altogether outside the jurisdiction of logic. With one breath they say: Aristotle is useless, because the "Organon" could never have led men to discover the stomach-pump; and with the next breath they ask you what you mean by admiring the "Ode on a Grecian Urn" if you can't give any logical reason for your admiration. Your religion doesn't rest on a logical foundation, they say. But does anything of any consequence rest on a logical foundation? Can you reduce the "Morte d'Arthur" into valid syllogisms in Barbara, can you "disprove" Salisbury Cathedral by the aid of Celarent. What is the "rational" explanation of our wonder and joy at the vision of the hills? Are a great symphony, the swell and triumph of the organ, the voices of the choristers, to be tested by the process of the understanding? But perhaps I am misjudging the people who ask these questions. When they say that logic does not discover truth, they doubtless mean by logic that formal analysis of the ratiocinative process that is rightly so called; but I am inclined to think that when they condemn religious or artistic emotions because they are "illogical," they mean by "illogical" that which does not conduce to the ease and comfort of the digestive apparatus or the money-making faculty. They are terrible fellows, you know, some of these persons. For example, I asked, with a tone of undue triumph, I am afraid, for the "reason why" we experience awe and delight in the presence of the hills. But in certain quarters my problem would be very quickly solved. I should be told, more in sorrow than in anger, that my emotion at the sight of certain shapes of earth was due to the fact that hill air was highly ozonised, and that the human race had acquired an instinctive pleasure in breathing it, greatly to its digestive profit. And if I tried to turn the tables by declaring that I experienced an equal, though a different delight in the spectacle of a desolate, smoking marsh, where a red sun sinks from a world of shivering reeds, I suppose I should hear that some remote ancestor of mine had found in some such place "pterodactyls plentiful and strong on the wing." And if I like the woods, it was because a monkey sat at the root of my family tree, and if I love an ancient garden it is because I am "second cousin to the worm."

There: I confess it is difficult to keep one's temper with these people, but one must try to do so. Do you remember how Trunnion's marriage was delayed? The bridegroom set out bravely with his retinue for the parish-church, where the bride waited a whole half hour—in vain. A messenger was sent who saw:

"The whole troop disposed in a long field, crossing the road obliquely, and headed by the bridegroom and his friend Hatchway, who finding himself hindered by a hedge from proceeding farther in the same direction, fired a pistol and stood over to the other side, making an obtuse angle with the line of his former course; and the rest of the squadron followed his example, keeping always in the rear of each other like a flight of wild geese.

"Surprised at this strange method of journeying, the messenger came up ... and desired he would proceed with more expedition. To this message Mr Trunnion replied, 'Hark ye, brother, don't you see we make all possible speed? Go back, and tell those who sent you, that the wind has shifted since we weighed anchor, and that we are obliged to make short trips in tacking, by reason of the narrowness of the channel; and that, as we lie within six points of the wind, they must make some allowance for variation and leeway.' 'Lord, sir!' said the valet, 'what occasion have you to go zig-zag in that manner? Do but clap spurs to your horses, and ride straight forward, and I'll engage you shall be at the church porch in less than a quarter of an hour.' 'What! right in the wind's eye?' answered the commander. 'Ahey! brother, where did you learn your navigation?'"

You see Commodore Trunnion's "logic" was perfect, only it was the logic of seamanship and not of riding to church on horseback. There are a good many people at the present day who are quite unable to get to church in time, for "reasons" as valid as Trunnion's; and when I hear of "the scientific basis of literature" I am always a little reminded of those scarecrows straggling in short tacks from one side of the lane to the other on their way to the wedding. The moral is, you know, that they didn't get there.

I tackled a materialist once on very similar lines. He began by saying that time and thought devoted to religion (they never see that art and religion stand or fall together, religion being the foundation of the fine arts) were an utter waste of time as they only diverted us from consideration of the present world, which we ought to study to the utmost; and he went on to praise some saying of Confucius on the folly of troubling about the future things. Then I went for him. He had to admit that agriculture is good, and I pointed out to him that England was changed from a savage wilderness into a pleasant garden by the monastic houses. He agreed that to found and endow hospitals and alms-houses was not precisely a waste of time, and I showed him that such institutions were begun by the religion of the past and carried on by the religion of the present. Then he allowed, in response to my Socratic question, that painting was something, and I demonstrated that all painting arose from the religious impulse, that the greatest paintings in the world were meant to adorn churches. Then he admitted the value of architecture, and he got the Parthenon, all the mediæval cathedrals, and the wonderful mound temples of Ceylon right at his head. He granted me that travel civilised, and I rubbed in the pilgrimage; he confessed that he liked to read the Latin and Greek classics—sometimes—and he received from me information as to the monastic scriptorium, and its part in the preservation of the old literature. As for the blessedness of forming one's character on the teaching of Confucius; there happened to be an article in the morning's paper on the Mandarin class! Well, my rationalist hadn't anything to say to it at all, with the exception of some vague remark that the Romans made roads, which, considering the state of England in the sixth century, was about as helpful as the somewhat similar remark of Mr F's. Aunt—that there are milestones on the Dover Road. I told him that the only Roman civilisation which contributed to the making of our country was that brought over by St Austin; and he had to allow that his statement that religion was a waste of time, an elaborate form of idleness, was, to put it mildly, not proven. Then he said kindly but firmly that religion wasn't rational, and I used up most of the arguments that I have used to-night; I mean, I showed him that it is good to paint pictures, to write poems, to devise romances, and to compose symphonies, and that it is also good to meditate and enjoy all these things. Hence, he was forced to admit, that his suppressed premiss had been disproved, and that he must no longer say: "that which is not rational is absurd."

And then, I think, the fun really began. I carried the war into the very camp of the enemy; that is, into actual, observable life, into the every day world of fact and experience. You talk about "reason," I said, and I presume you won't mind if I substitute, occasionally, "common sense" for reason, as I think that in your phraseology the two terms are very fairly equated. Very well, then, don't you think that there is a good deal of common sense in many of the actions of animals? Take the case of the small birds who mob an owl all day, in order that their enemy may be kept awake, and so unable to hoot at night. Take the case of the ants, who milk the aphides, and go slave-hunting. Take the bees, who rise to an emergency, and remedy, with singular contrivance, the threatened lack of a queen. Take the dog, who brought a wounded fellow to the hospital where he had been cured. All these are instances of common sense, aren't they, as rational as the telegram "Sell Cobras at once"? Very good; animals, then, have a plentiful supply of reason, and not of a mere mechanical reason, but of reason that can rise to the height of unforeseen cases, and remedy unexpected evils. When the experimenter tilted the bees' house to one side, so that the equilibrium was in danger, a sufficient number of bees climbed up, and placed themselves on the other side so that they constituted a balance; here there was no mechanism, but a calculated and rational contrivance. Animals, then, have reason and its effect artifice; the adaptation of means to secure ends. But, then, how about instinct? By what motion does the swallow make her nest in spring? Can the bee demonstrate the advantages of the hexagon cell? Does the fly, laying its eggs, here and there, in this or in that according to its kind, in meat or in dung, or in the crevices of a wall, rationally foresee that it is providing for the future grub its only possible food? No; but then animals, even, perform "irrational" actions; though they have common sense they do things which must be troublesome to them, at some instance, which is not common sense. But if a bluebottle lays her eggs in my beef, and knows not why, perhaps I, a man, may sing the Sanctus, and pray that I may be joined cum angelis et archangelis, cum thronis et dominationbus, Cumque omni militiâ cælestis exercitus.

And consider our own human life; the great coups of war, commerce, diplomacy, of all the conduct of life, are often, or usually, the result of "intuitions," that is of irrational and inexplicable mental processes, which elude all analysis. If the knowledge, the successful and triumphant knowledge of men and affairs and strategy were a "rational" product; then, indeed, Carlyle's dictum were true, and each one of us were, at choice, a man of genius in diplomacy, or business, or battle. We know that it is not so, and that no man by taking thought can make himself, say, a Stonewall Jackson. And we have all heard of the "woman's reason" — "I don't know why I am sure that $x = a$, but I am sure" — and this extremely irrational process often corresponds with the truth. So, I finished up, your "reason" far from being the despot of the world, turns out to be a humble, though useful, deputy-assistant councillor-general, and is by no means a prerogative force, even in affairs of common, everyday existence. Why, "reason," alone and unassisted, won't enable you to make a decent living by selling ribbons and laces, and you have been trying to make me accept its dictation in the highest affairs of the soul. You have been appealing from the King's Majesty in Council to the Magistrates of Little Pedlington in Petty Sessions assembled!

Then my rationalist made a point. You know, he said, that some men seem to have an almost miraculous skill in solving mathematical problems: would you, therefore, give up teaching the ordinary arithmetic? I was not alarmed; I pointed out that the analogy was not quite perfect. The case, I said, was this. A certain number of "problems" were, confessedly, beyond the jurisdiction of the "ordinary arithmetic" altogether, but offered no difficulties to the "lightning calculator," who obtained results that were demonstratively correct, and I therefore thought it well to trust to him in all problems of a similar character, even though the "ordinary arithmetic," confessedly incompetent, assured me that his answers were wholly unreliable—a case of a schoolboy, well on in Colenso, scouting the Binomial Theorem because one couldn't prove it by Practice or the Rule of Three. I left then, unanswered, and I suppose my friend passed the rest of the evening in showing that Salisbury Cathedral was "opposed" to the facts of Biology, and that Sisters of Charity are to be classed with criminal lunatics.

But, you know, I was the real lunatic. You would not have "argued" with me if I had disparaged the Greek alphabet, because it never grilled a single steak; I hinted the course you would probably have pursued if I had chanced to make such an alarming remark. And why should I argue with the sect of Macaulay, with the tribe which utters such stuff as this:

"Assuredly if the tree which Socrates planted and Plato watered is to be judged of by its flowers and leaves, it is the noblest of trees. But if we take the homely test of Bacon—if we judge the tree by its fruits—our opinion of it may be less favourable. When we sum up the useful truths which we owe to that philosophy, to what do they amount.... But when we look for something more—for something which adds to the comfort or alleviates the calamities of the human race—we are forced to own ourselves disappointed."

No; there is, really, nothing to be said. If the Learned Pig found voice and articulate speech and expressed his scorn of the poet's art, since it added nothing to the pleasures of the wash-tub, we might wonder but we should not argue; and it were idle to contend with a Laughing Jackass, contemptuously amused by the chanting of the cathedral choir.

And, perhaps, you are wondering what all this talk of mine has to do with our main subject—literature? But don't you see that all the while I have merely been reiterating our old conclusions in a new phraseology? I may have appeared to you to be the last of the Cavaliers, gallantly contending for the rights of Holy Church, but, in reality, I have been showing, at every step, that Jane Austen's works are not literature. Yes, but it is so. If the science of life, if philosophy, consisted of a series of mathematical propositions, capable of rational demonstration, then, "Pride and Prejudice" would be the highest pinnacle of the literary art; but if not, but oh! if we, being wondrous, journey through a wonderful world, if all our joys are from above, from the other world where the Shadowy Companion walks, then no mere making of the likeness of the external shape will be our art, no veracious document will be our truth; but to us, initiated, the Symbol will be offered, and we shall take the Sign and adore, beneath the outward and perhaps unlovely accidents, the very Presence and eternal indwelling of God.

We have tracked Ecstasy by many strange paths, in divers strange disguises, but I think that now, and only now, we have discovered its full and perfect definition. For Artifice is of Time, but Art is of Eternity.

APPENDIX

Poe was not altogether right in saying that the object of poetry was Beauty as distinguished from Truth. I don't for a moment suppose that his meaning was amiss, but I hardly like his expression of it. I should contend, on the other hand, that poetry κατ' ἐξοχήν, and literature, generally, are the sole media by which the very highest truth can be conveyed. Poe, no doubt, meant to state a proposition which is true and self-evident—that poetry has nothing to do with scientific truth, or facts, or information of any kind, and I say that that proposition is self-evident, because we have already seen that in literature, facts as facts, have no existence at all. They are only "words" in the language of literary art, and are used as symbols of something else. That A. is in love with B. is a "scientific truth," a fact; but if it be not also a symbol, it has no literary existence whatever; and this of course is what Poe wished to say—literature is not a matter of information.

But I doubt, after all, whether Poe had quite grasped the theory of literature, of all the arts. You remember that he says that he yields to no man in his love of the truth; and unless he meant the highest truth the statement is almost nonsensical. No one, I should imagine, surely not Poe, would express his enthusiasm for facts as facts, would adore correct information in the abstract. You remember what Rossetti said—that he neither knew nor cared whether the sun went round the earth or the earth round the sun—and so far as art is concerned this is, no doubt, the expression of the true faith, which, from what we know of Poe, would be his faith also. We should therefore conclude that by truth he meant philosophical truth, the highest truth, the essential truth as distinguished from the accidental, the universal as distinguished from the particular. Yet in the next breath he contrasts this Truth with Beauty, being clearly under the impression that they were two different things. Of course he was completely mistaken. In the last analysis it is entirely true that "Beauty is Truth and Truth Beauty": they are one and the same entity seen from different points of view. You will see how this fits in with all we have been saying about literature lately: how we can if we please put our test of literature into yet another phraseology. For instance: "Vanity Fair" is information, while "Pickwick" is Truth; the one tells you a number of facts about Becky Sharpe and other people, while the other symbolises certain eternal and essential elements in human nature by means of incidents. And, as I said, it is doubtful whether truth in this, its highest and its real significance, can be adequately expressed in any other way. All the profound verities which have been revealed to man have come to him under the guise of myths and symbols—such as the myth of Dionysus—and truth in the form of a mathematical demonstration or a "rational" statement is a contradiction in terms. Yet note the profound vice of language; we are obliged to use the same word to imply things which are separated by an immeasurable gulf. It is "true" that Mrs Stickings sent away Ethelberta to-night (you imparted that interesting fact, and I rely on your testimony), and the "Don Quixote" is "true": that is, it conveys to us by means of symbols the verities of our own nature.

But Poe had not grasped the essential distinction between literature and "literature." He thought that poetry alone should be beautiful, or as we should say, ecstatic; he did not see that the qualities which make poetry to be what it is must also be present in prose if it is to be something more than "reading-matter." Poetry of course is literature in its purest state; it is, as I think I once said, almost the soul without the body; at its highest it is almost pure art unmixed with the alloy of artifice. And to carry on the analysis, the finest form of poetry is necessarily the lyrical. Where you get the element of narrative, you are apt also to get the element of prose; there have to be passages linking the raptures together, and these will, probably or indeed necessarily, run on lower levels.

Of course primitive man had moods in which rapture seemed to embrace everything, to invest every detail of existence with its own singular and inexplicable glory. A meal by the seashore, the dry wood flaming and crackling on the sand, the roasting goat's flesh, the honey-sweet wine, dark and almost as glorious as the sea itself—a mere dinner of half-savages, one might think it, but it too seems to have its solemnity and its inner meaning. I believe this element in the early poetry has often been noticed; people have wondered at the naïve delight with which the writers describe the work of man's hands, and they are, I think, inclined to account for it on the ground that then everything was new. This might pass, perhaps, since as you, no doubt, perceive, "everything new" means "everything unknown" (that which is known is no longer new), but I hardly think that the explanation can stand in its present form. I am not at all up in the theories which assign this or that age to the appearance of man on the earth, but I presume that on the gentlest and most antiquated computation man must have long known the world before Homer wrote; so one scarcely sees that human skill and art, the knack of making things and the gift of adorning them, could have been novelties, or in any sense, "things unknown." I repeat I know nothing or next to nothing about these dates in anthropology, but one has heard something about the neolithic age, and the palæolithic age, about the very early man who scratched the rude likeness of a reindeer on the brute's own bone, and so

110

there hardly seems room for this theory of novelty. And besides, as we have seen, the rapture is universal or all but universal; it colours the whole of life, including the meal by the seashore; and there, we see, there was no possibility of invention or sense of newness. No; the theory is tempting, and it would fall in perfectly, as I daresay you see, with all that we have concluded about literature, but I really think that it must be definitely abandoned. No; it seems to me that primitive man, Homeric man, mediæval man, man, indeed, almost to our own day when the School Board (and other things) have got hold of him, had such an unconscious but all-pervading, all-influencing conviction that he was a wonderful being, descended of a wonderful ancestry, and surrounded by mysteries of all kinds, that even the smallest details of his life partook of the ruling ecstasy; he was so sure that he was miraculous that it seemed that no part of his life could escape from the miracle, so that to him every meal became a sacrament.

It is the attitude of the primitive man, of the real man, of the child, always and everywhere; it may be briefly summed up in the phrase: things are because they are wonderful. This, of course, is the atmosphere in which poets ought to live, and in which poetry should be produced. Formerly it was natural to all men or almost all; now, perhaps, it has to be regained by a conscious effort; and the difficulty of the effort, the impossibility of sustaining it for long, explain the supremacy of lyrical poetry. If you lived in a world that could regard a common meal as a sacrament, you could be supreme in narrative poetry; but, that atmosphere wanting, we have to be content for the most part with the lyric, with the simple incantation, without any description of the circumstance or occasion.

Yet prose, though it yields in much to the world, must still keep the same ideal before it as poetry. I say, distinctly, that the only essential, defining difference between the two is to be sought in the "numbering" of poetry, in the fact that art, in its intensest raptures, in its most truly "natural" moment, desires and obtains the strictest and most formal laws. It is, I suppose, immaterial what these laws are, rhyme, assonance, accents, feet, alliteration, all testify to the important and essential rule that freedom is chiefly free when it is most bound and bounded by restrictions which we should call artificial, which are, in truth, in the highest sense, natural. And this, I am sure, is the only possible distinction that can be established between such a book as the "Odyssey" and such a book as the "Morte d'Arthur." Neither is "prosaic" in the common sense of the word; each is "poetical"; but the Greek book is poetry because it is numbered, and the English is prose because it lacks number. Of course there are difficult cases; hybrids, as there always are, whatever laws one may lay down.

That word "natural" is another of the many traps that language sets us. I think that its real meaning has become almost reversed. Take the average man to church, and ask him his opinion of the "intoning," and in nine cases out of ten he will say that it may be pretty, but that it is very unnatural. He means, of course, that speaking is natural, and that singing—"numerosity" of tone—is not natural, is, in a word, artificial. He is utterly wrong. It is artificial to speak in the ordinary manner, while the priests' chant, and every chant are purely natural. For the proof of this you have only to read a little—a very little—about primitive, or "natural" peoples, or, more simply, to listen to children at play. You will always find that where convention has not cast out nature, some kind of "sing-song," some sort of chant is the entirely natural utterance of man in his most fervent, that is, his most natural moments. Listen to half-a-dozen children (children, you must remember, are all "primitives" and therefore natural) playing some game, learning their lesson at school. Their voices are pretty sure to fall into a very rude, but a distinctly measured, chant. The Greek drama was intoned, the Koran is intoned, the Welsh preacher of to-day at the impassioned height of eloquence begins to chant, the Persian passion-plays are recited in a sing-song. Nay, but listen only to our great tragic actor. Quite unconsciously, I am sure, he has elaborated for himself a distinctly musical and measured utterance, so that a skilful musician, provided with scored paper, could note Irving's delivery of many passages, as if it were music. The Chinese language, I am told, depends largely on the tonal variations which distinguish the meaning of one word from that of another; you will find the same thing in the Norwegian; and the Jewish "cantillation," which is "sing-song" in a very simple form, bears witness to the truth—that "speaking" is acquired, conventional, and artificial, while "singing" is natural. All this would be perfectly clear in itself, would require no demonstration of any kind, if it were not for the fact that we have, somehow or other, got into the way of making the very impudent assumption that man is only natural when he is doing business on the Stock-Exchange or reading leading-articles. It seems almost too nonsensical an assumption to put into words, but I really do believe that "at the back of our heads" there is a sort of vague, floating idea that there never were any real men at all till the period of the first Reform Bill, and I suppose that before very long Lord John Russell will be pushed back into the region of myth, and the foundation of the School Board will be the era of true humanity. I say, this sounds too ridiculous, but examine yourself and see whether you don't dimly believe that before the advent of trousers the whole world was really "play-acting," that existence in the days of laced coats was, in a way, a kind of phantasmagoria, and that a man who wore chain-mail was hardly a man. I believe it really is so, and you will find the same nonsense influencing religious opinion. Take your average Protestant, and I am much mistaken if you do not discover that he believes some grotesque preacher, in his greasy black suit, mouthing platitudes at his conventicle to be somehow more "natural" than the priest, clad in the mystical robes of his office, chanting Mass at the altar. But in literature—why this perversion of the word influences the whole of criticism. Jane Austen, we say, is natural, and Edgar Allan Poe is unnatural, or as it is sometimes expressed, inhuman. Of course, if you wish for the truth, the proposition must be reversed, unless you are willing to believe that a Company Prospectus is, somehow, more natural and more human than, say, Tennyson's "Fatima." If you think that the real man is the stomach, there is, of course, an end of the discussion; but then we should have to admit that all the greatest artists of the world were maniacs. But you see clearly, don't you, that all these questions as to what we shall get for dinner, and whom shall we meet at dinner, and in what order shall we go into dinner, and how shall we behave at dinner, are in no sense natural, since they are all so purely temporary, since they will be answered by one age in a manner that will seem wholly "unnatural" to the next. That, I think, is truly natural which is unchanging, which belongs to men always, at all times, and in all ages. In this sense, ecstasy is natural to man, and it finds expression in the arts, in poetry, in romance, in singing, in melody, in dancing, in painting, in architecture. Many animals have sufficient artifice to shelter themselves from the weather, no animal has architecture, or the art of beauty in building; many animals, or all animals, have the faculty of communicating with one another by means of signs, but man alone has the art of language.

Has it ever struck you while I have been talking of ecstasy in books, that it is nearly always a question of degree, of more or less? I think I indicated as much while I was talking about "Pickwick"; I showed how the ecstatic conception had been alloyed with much baser matter, in other words that there was much in "Pickwick" that was by no means literature. And, I daresay, though I am not sure, that if you were to go through your Meredith you might succeed in finding some passages and sentences which are literature, and for all I know there may be hints of rapture between the lines of "Pride and Prejudice." Still, we do not call a man poet on the strength of a single line.

But sometimes one is confronted with books which are really very difficult to judge, and this sometimes happens because the ecstasy, the true literary feeling, supposing it to be present, is present not here or there, not in a phrase or in a particular passage, but throughout, in a very weak solution, if one may borrow the phraseology of physical science. We read such books, and are puzzled, feeling that, somehow, they are literature, only we can't say why, since on the face of it they seem only to be entertaining reading. Do you know that I can conceive many people who would find something of this difficulty in Mark Twain's "Huckleberry Finn"? Here you have a tale of the rude America of forty or fifty years ago, of a Mississippi village, full of the most ordinary people, of a boy and a negro who "run away." I don't think anyone with the slightest perception of literature could read it without experiencing extraordinary delight, but I can imagine many people would be a good deal puzzled to justify the pleasure they had received. The "stuff" of the book is so very common and commonplace, isn't it, it seems so frankly a rough bit of recollection drawn up from the author's boyish days with jottings added from the time when he was a pilot on one of the river-boats—it is all so apparently devoid of "literary" feeling that I am sure many a reader must have felt greatly ashamed of his huge enjoyment. To me "Huckleberry Finn" is not a very difficult case. That flight by night down the great unknown, rolling river, between the dim marshy lands and the high "bluffs" of the other shore comes in my mind well under the great "Odyssey" class; it has, indeed, the old, unquenchable joy of wandering into the unknown in a more acute degree than "Pickwick," which, as we have seen, is to be reckoned under the same heading. In a word it is pure romance, and you will note that the story is told by a boy, and that by this method a larger element of wonder is secured, for even in this absurd age children are allowed to be amazed at the spectacle of the world. In the mouth of a man the tale would necessarily have lost somewhat of its "strangeness," since partly from affectation, partly from vicious training, partly from the absorption of the "getting-on" process, grown-up people have largely succeeded in quenching the sense of mystery which should be their principal delight. You have only to read the average book of travels to see how this affectation (or perversion of the soul) has deprived the seeing being of his sight. Dip into a book—say a book on China—and you will probably find that Pekin streets are dusty in summer and muddy in winter, and that the author caught cold through imprudent bathing. So it is well for us that Mark Twain put his story in the mouth of an "infant," who is frankly at liberty to express his sense of the marvels of the world. Later, there is an introduction of the "literary" feeling; those chapters about Jim's "Evasion" are very Cervantic in their artifice and method, but, to my thinking, they have lost the spirit, though they preserve the body. They are most amusing reading, but they are burlesque and nothing more than burlesque; and from them one can almost imagine what "Don Quixote" would have been if it had been written by a very clever man, by an artificer who was not an artist. But the earlier chapters are wonderfully fine, and I think that it would be difficult to find a more successful rendering of the old "wandering" theme with modern language.

But there is another writer who is much more difficult to account for—I mean Miss Wilkins. I confess I find her tales delightful, and I often read them, but as you know I am not content to rest on my own pleasure in literary criticism. We are no longer talking of the great masterpieces, of the gigantic achievements of such men as Homer, Sophocles, Rabelais, Cervantes; we agreed that when we spoke of these great, enduring miracles of art, it was best to lay aside all question of liking or not liking, of reading often or reading seldom. But when one comes to modern days, to books which have yet to prove their merit by the test of their endurance, it is pardonable if one is sometimes a little confused, if one fails to discriminate at once between the merely interesting and the really artistic. I may be so delighted with a book for reasons that have nothing to do with art, that, by an unconscious trick of the mind, I persuade myself that I am reading literature while there is only reading-matter. And at one time I was inclined to think that I had "confused" Miss Wilkins in this manner. For, on the surface, you have in her books merely village tales of New Englanders, tales often sentimental, often trivial enough, and sometimes, it would seem, of hardly more than local interest. Hardly can one conceive the possibility of any ecstasy in these pleasant stories; for they deal, ostentatiously, with the surface of things, with a breed of Englishmen whose chief pride it was to hide away and smother all those passions and emotions which are the peculiar mark of man as man.

Yet, I believe that I can justify my love of Miss Wilkins's work on a higher ground than that of mere liking. In the first place I agree with Mr T. P. O'Connor, who pointed out very well that the passion does come through the reserve, and occasionally in the most volcanic manner. He selects a scene from "Pembroke," in which the young people play at some dancing game called "Copenhagen," and Mr O'Connor shows that though the boys and girls of Pembroke knew nothing of it, they were really animated by the spirit of the Bacchanals, that the fire and glow of passion, of the youthful ecstasy, burst through all the hard crusts of Calvinism and New England reserve. And we have agreed that if a writer can make passion for us, if he can create the image of the eternal human ecstasy, we have agreed that in such a case the writer is an artist.

But I think that there are other things, more subtle, more delicately hinted things in Miss Wilkins's tales; or rather I should say that they are all pervaded and filled with an emotion, which I can hardly think that the writer has realised. Well, I find it difficult to express exactly what I mean, but I think that the whole impression which one receives from these tales is one of loneliness, of isolation. Compare Miss Wilkins with Jane Austen, the New England stories with "Pride and Prejudice." You might imagine, at first, that in one case as in the other there is a sense of retirement, of separation from the world, that Miss Austen's heroines are as remote from the great streams and whirlpools of life as any "Jane Field" or Charlotte of Massachusetts. But in reality this is not so. The people in the English novels are in no sense remote; they are merely dull; they cannot be remote, indeed, since they are not human beings at all but merely the representatives of certain superficial manners and tricks of manner which were common in the rural England of ninety years ago. "Remoteness" is an affection of the soul, and wicker-figures, dressed up in the clothes of a period, cannot have any such affections predicated of them; and consequently though Emma or Elizabeth may appear very quaint to us from the contrast between the manners of the 'tens and the 'nineties, they cannot be remote. But that does seem to me the quality of those books of Miss Wilkins's; the people appear to be very far off from the world, to live in an isolated sphere, and each one lives his own life, and dwells apart with his own soul, and in spite of all the trivial chatter and circumstance of the village one feels that each is a human being moved by eminently human affections.

It seems to me that one of the most important functions of literature is to seize the really fine flavours of life and to preserve them, as it were, in permanent form. When we were talking about "Huckleberry Finn," for example, I remember that I spoke of it as the story of a boy who "runs away." But what a curious magic there is in these words "runs away." Doesn't it, when you come to examine the phrase, exhale the very essence and spirit of romance? Some time ago I reminded you that the essential thing is concealed under all manner of grotesque and unseemly forms, that one can detect a veritable human passion under the cry of the news-boy, shouting, "All the winners!" So I think that phrase, "run away," carries to us its meaning and significance. For, after all, what did all the heroes of romance do but "run away"? They left the region of the known, the familiar fields or the familiar shores, and adventured out in the great waste of the unexplored, into the forest or upon the sea. Here, perhaps, you have the true interpretation of the phrase "divine discontent," for surely only that is divine which revolts from the commonness of the common life, which is conscious of things beyond, of better things, of a world which transcends all daily experience. I said once, I think, that the English passion for trading goes very well with the supremacy of English poetry, since poetry and shop-keeping are but different expressions of the one idea; and here again you find confirmation of the theory in that very marked English characteristic—the desire of wandering, of "going on and on" in the manner of a knight errant or a fairy tale hero. Of course, in practice, this really divine impulse is corrupted by all kinds of earthly, secondary motions; and just as the love of a venture which is at the root of trade often or always ends in a very vulgar wish to make money and more money and to set up a brougham and confound the Smiths, so the great joy of exploration, of running away from the mapped and charted land has for its issues the "development of markets," the "progress of civilisation," the profitable sale of poison, and all manner of base and blackguardly manœuvres. But, of course, one expects all this; it is the inevitable mixture of the lower with the higher which characterises all our human ways. Still the higher motive dwells within us—I suspect, indeed, that if it were not for the higher the lower could hardly flourish—and so when you hear that a boy has run away to sea or elsewhere I wish you to think kindly of him as a survival of the most primitive and important human passions. Yes, I think I am right in saying that the lower things of humanity only flourish in consequence of the existence of the higher. Take the French nation, for example. It is infinitely more bent on gain for the mere sake of gain than the English; it is ready to work harder, to give more time, to live more unpleasantly, to eat less and to drink less than the English; and all in the pursuit of money. Rationally, in short, the French should be infinitely better men of business than the English; and yet we know that this is not so, that the English is, par excellence, the business nation. Seriously, I believe, that this is so because the French are money-grubbers and nothing more, because they hate a "risk" of any kind, because they abhor any kind of mercantile venturing into the unknown. In other words, they engage in money-making simply for the sake of making money: they have no joy of the hazard, they will never deserve the title of "merchant adventurers," and, therefore, they remain in truth a nation of shopkeepers and of second-rate shopkeepers. Sir, a man of acute intelligence would, in the seventeenth century, have deduced the future state of French and English commerce, of French and English colonization from a comparison between Shakespeare and Racine. I have no doubt that the Phœnicians were shopkeepers of the French kind, and hence their extinction, their shadowy survival merely in the history of their conquerors.

You think the Roman Empire a formidable objection to my theory, because Roman literature and Roman art show, in general, so little of the imaginative, adventurous faculty? I think the objection is formidable, but I believe that it can be redargued, as Dominie Sampson used to say. The Roman Empire was such a purely military settlement, wasn't it? it was, if one may say so, a garrisoning of the world, not in any way a real colonizing in the Greek and the English sense. And in the second place, do you know that I have grave doubts whether we know very much of the Roman spirit from the Roman literature. How far into the English character would the works of the excellent Dr. Johnson carry us? One hardly finds Chaucer, the Elizabethans, the Cavalier poets, Keats or Wordsworth in "Rasselas" and "The Rambler," and I have always suspected that Latin literature was in a great measure "Johnsonized," periwigged, hidden and perverted by the irresistible flood of Greek culture. It may be a paradox, but I have a very strong conviction that the Missal and the Breviary tell us more about the true Latin character than Cicero and Horace. But we must be thankful that in the sixteenth and early seventeenth centuries

121

England stood aloof from the continent of Europe, and that when it did borrow it transformed and transmuted so that the original entirely lost its foreign character. I always think that change of Madame de Querouaille into Madam Carewell such a wonderful instance of our nationalism—our transforming force! If it had been otherwise, if we had grovelled before the literature of France or Spain or Italy, as Rome grovelled before the literature of Greece— well, perhaps, English literature would have meant "Chevy Chace" and a few old ballads, and the eighteenth century! I hate the Reformation, but perhaps it saved our literature, simply by isolating the nation.

I claimed, I think, literary merit for Miss Wilkins because her books give out an impression of loneliness. I think that is so, but I should like to point out that "loneliness" is merely another synonym for that one property which makes the difference between real literature and reading-matter. If you look into the French literature of the last two hundred years and complain of its elegant nothingness, of its wholly secondary character, I would point out that it is second-rate because it is the expression, not of the lonely human soul, like a star, dwelling apart, but of society, of the ruelles, of the salon, of polite company, of the café and the boulevard. I am not making an accusation, I am adopting the terms of the eminent M. de Brunetière, who tells us, I think, that French literature is beautiful because it is firstly sociable, and secondly because it is a kind of a long "talk to ladies." I hardly think that I need go into the merits of the question; you and I, I take it, are convinced of the vast immeasurable inferiority of Racine to Shakespeare (with these two names one sums up the whole debate), but I am quite sure that M. de Brunetière has given the true reason of the French literature being on the distinctly low level. It is always Thackeray, it is always

Pope, it is always Jane Austen; it is, in our sense of the word, not literature at all, though, to be sure, its artifice is often of the most exquisite description. Of course I do not speak of the ultimate reason—that is to be sought, I presume, in the mental constitution of the nation—but when one reads M. de Brunetière's account of the formation of modern French letters, and notes his insistance on the social element as the chief factor, one may be pretty sure that this social factor is responsible for the pleasant nullities which we all know. You may feel pretty certain, I think, that real literature has always been produced by men who have preserved a certain loneliness of soul, if not of body; the masterpieces are not generated by that pleasant and witty traffic of the drawing-rooms, but by the silence of the eternal hills. Remember; we have settled that literature is the expression of the "standing out," of the withdrawal of the soul, it is the endeavour of every age to return to the first age, to an age, if you like, of savages, when a man crept away to the rocks or to the forests that he might utter, all alone, the secrets of his own soul.

So this is my plea for Miss Wilkins. I think that she has indicated this condition of "ecstasis"; she has painted a society, indeed, but a society in which each man stands apart, responsible only for himself and to himself, conscious only of himself and his God. You will note this, if you read her carefully, you will see how this doctrine of awful, individual loneliness prevails so far that it is carried into the necessary and ordinary transactions of social life, often with results that are very absurd. Many of the people in her stories are so absolutely convinced of their "loneliness," so certain that there are only two persons in the whole universe—each man and his God—that they do not shrink from transgressing and flouting all the social orders and regulations, in spite of their very

123

strong and social instinct drawing them in the opposite direction. You remember the man who vowed that under certain circumstances he would sit on the meeting-house steps every Sunday? He kept his vow—for ten years I think—and he kept it in spite of his profound horror of ridicule, of doing what other people didn't do, in spite of his own happiness; but he kept it because he realised his "loneliness," because he saw quite clearly that he must stand or fall by his own word and his own promise, and that the opinions of others could be of no possible importance to him. The instance is ludicrous, even to the verge of farce, and yet I call it a witness to the everlasting truth that, at last, each man must stand or fall alone, and that if he would stand, he must, to a certain extent, live alone with his own soul. It is from this mood of lonely reverie and ecstasy that literature proceeds, and I think that the sense of all this is diffused throughout Miss Wilkins's New England stories.

You ask me for a new test—or rather for a new expression of the one test—that separates literature from the mass of stuff which is not literature. I will give you a test that will startle you; literature is the expression, through the æsthetic medium of words, of the dogmas of the Catholic Church, and that which in any way is out of harmony with these dogmas is not literature. Yes, it is really so; but not exactly in the sense which you suppose. No literal compliance with Christianity is needed, no, nor even an acquaintance with the doctrines of Christianity. The Greeks, celebrating the festivals of Dionysus, Cervantes recounting the fooleries of Don Quixote, Dickens measuring Mr Pickwick's glasses of cold punch, Rabelais with his thirsty Pantagruel were all sufficiently Catholic from our point of view, and the cultus of Aphrodite is merely a symbol misunderstood and possibly corrupted, and if you can describe an initiatory dance of savages in the proper manner, I shall call you a good Catholic. You say that "Robert Elsmere" is not literature, and you are perfectly right, but I hope you don't condemn it because it contains arguments directed against the Catholic Faith? These, from our own standpoint, are simply nothing at all, not reckoning either way. We pass them over, just as we should pass over a passage on quadratic equations pleasantly interpolated by an author into the body of his romance. The conscious opinions of a writer are simply not worth twopence in the court of literature; who cares to enquire into the theology of Keats? But when we find not only the consciousness but also the subconsciousness permeated by the impression that man is a logical, "rationalistic" creature and nothing more, when the total impression of the human being gathered from the book is of a simply demonstrating and demonstrable animal; then, we may be perfectly assured that we have not to deal with literature. It is the subconsciousness, remember, alone that matters; and (to put it again theologically) you will find that books which are not literature proceed from ignorance of the Sacramental System. Thackeray was an unconscious heretic, while George Eliot was a conscious one, but each was ignorant of the meaning of Sacramentalism, and so, making allowance for the fact that the one was a clever man, while the other was a dull, industrious woman, you have from each a view of life that is substantially the same, and entirely false. Each was profoundly convinced that there are milestones on the Dover Road, and each, in his several way, was so intent on the truth of this proposition (and it is a perfectly true one) that the secret of the scenery and the secret of Canterbury Cathedral are altogether to seek in their books. Certainly the gentleman is a delightful companion, and the milestones seem few indeed while we are on the way, while with the other guide we feel like a girls' school, compelled to listen to the "now, young ladies" and the "lessons" which every object on the road suggests. Still, the total view is much the same, the same in genus if not in species, and you may add Flaubert to your companions on the road and you will be in the same case. But read a chapter of "Don Quixote"; you will not be aware of the existence of the milestones, since your gaze is fixed on the mystery of the woods, and you are a pilgrim to the blissful shrine beyond. Don't imagine that you can improve your literary chances by subscribing the Catechism or the Decrees of the Council of Trent. No; I can give you no such short and easy plan for excelling; but I tell you that unless you have assimilated the final dogmas—the eternal truths—upon which those things rest, consciously if you please, but subconsciously of necessity, you can never write literature, however clever and amusing you may be. Think of it, and you will see that from the literary standpoint, Catholic dogma is merely the witness, under a special symbolism, of the enduring facts of human nature and the universe; it is merely the voice which tells us distinctly that man is not the creature of the drawing-room and the Stock Exchange, but a lonely awful soul confronted by the Source of all Souls, and you will realise that to make literature it is necessary to be, at all events, subconsciously Catholic.

Have you noticed how many of the greatest writers, so far from desiring that compliment of "fidelity to life" do their best to get away from life, to make their books, in ordinary phraseology, "unreal?" I do not know whether anybody has compared the facts before or made the only possible inference from them; but you remember how Rabelais professes to derive his book from a little mouldy manuscript, found in a tomb, how Cervantes, beginning in propria persona authoris, breaks off and discovers the true history of "Don Quixote" in the Arabic Manuscript of Cid Hamet Benengeli, how Hawthorne prologises with the custom-house at Salem, and lights, in an old lumber-room, on the documents telling him the history of the "Scarlet Letter." "Pickwick" was a transcript of the "Transactions" or "Papers" of the Pickwick Club, and Tennyson's "Morte D'Arthur" shelters itself, in the same way, behind the personality of an imaginary writer. There is a very profound significance in all this, and you find a trace of the same instinct in the Greek Tragedies where the final scene, the peripeteia, is not shown on the stage, but described by a "messenger." The fact is that the true artist, so far from being the imitator of life, endures some of his severest struggles in endeavouring to get away from life, and until he can do this he knows that his labour is all in vain. It would be amusing to trace all the various devices which have been used to secure this effect of separation, of withdrawal from the common track of common things. I have just pointed out one, the hiding of the author, as it were, behind a mask, and in the Greek Play the analogous talking of what has happened in place of visibly showing it, but there must be many more. From this instinct I imagine arises the historical novel in all its forms, you make your story remote by placing it far back in time, by the exhibition of strange dresses and unfamiliar manners. Or again you may get virtually the same effect by using the remoteness of space, by playing on the theme "far, far away" which really calls up a very similar emotion to that produced by the other theme of "long, long ago," or "once on a time," as the fairy tale has it. Briefly we may say that all "strangeness" of incident, or plot, or style makes for this one end; and of course you see that all this is only the repetition of our old text in another form. It is, perhaps, hardly necessary to give the caution that, on the principle of corruptio optimi, there is nothing more melancholy than the book which has the body of fine literature without the soul, which uses literary methods without understanding. You needn't ask for proofs of that proposition; our memories are aghast with recollections of futile "historical novels," of the terrific school of the "two horsemen," and every Christmas brings its huge budget of those dreadful "boys' books," which carry commonplace to the very ends of the earth, and occasionally penetrate to the stars. And in style, too, what can be more depressing than the style which is meant to be "strange" and is only flatulent? In many cases of course such books as I have alluded to are mere survivals of tradition, conventions of bookmaking which bear witness to the fact that pirates and treasure-hoards were once symbols of wonder, and the extravagancies of style are probably to be accounted for in the same way. At some remote period it may, possibly, have been effective to call the sun, "the glorious orb," and even now some minds may be made to realise the strangeness of great flights of birds by the phrase "the feathered Zingari of the air"; but if one is a little sophisticated one feels the pathos and the futility of such efforts. The writer has felt and experienced the wonder of things—the beauty of the sun and the hieroglyphic mystery of the figures that the birds make in the air—and he feels, quite rightly, that to describe wonders one must suggest wonder by words. Unfortunately, he breaks down at this point, and falls back on unhappy phrases that give the very opposite impression to that which he wishes to excite. Here you have the whole history of "poetic diction." The instinct is in itself an entirely right one, and I need hardly say that the masters—those who have the secret—can use archaic forms, obsolete constructions, conventional phrases even, with miraculous effect. But the beginner would do well to be wary of these things, and to turn his face resolutely away from "flowery meads" and all the family of inversions. How is one to know when such phrases may be used? If I could give you the answer to that question I should be also giving you the secret of making literature, and from all our talks I expect you have gathered this much at all events—that the art of literature, with all the arts, is quite incommunicable. Many kinds of artifice, even, are unteachable—I could not write or be taught to write one of those George Eliot novels that I have been abusing with such hearty good will—but art is by its very definition quite without the jurisdiction of the schools, and the realm of the reasoning process, since art is a miracle, superior to the laws.